THE IMAGINARY
MAN

*Seven feisty women looking for someone
who can measure up*

SHORT STORIES BY SN WEDDLE

THE IMAGINARY
MAN

*Seven feisty women looking for someone
who can measure up*

SHORT STORIES BY SN WEDDLE

MEREO
Cirencester

Mereo Books

1A The Wool Market Dyer Street Cirencester Gloucestershire GL7 2PR
An imprint of Memoirs Publishing www.mereobooks.com

The imaginary man: 978-1-86151-703-6

First published in Great Britain in 2016
by Mereo Books, an imprint of Memoirs Publishing

Copyright ©2016

SN Weddle has asserted his right under the Copyright Designs and Patents Act 1988 to be identified as the author of this work.

This book is a work of fiction and except in the case of historical fact any resemblance to actual persons living or dead is purely coincidental.

A CIP catalogue record for this book is available from the British Library.

This book is sold subject to the condition that it shall not by way of trade or otherwise be lent, resold, hired out or otherwise circulated without the publisher's prior consent in any form of binding or cover, other than that in which it is published and without a similar condition, including this condition being imposed on the subsequent purchaser.

The address for Memoirs Publishing Group Limited can be found at
www.memoirspublishing.com

The Memoirs Publishing Group Ltd Reg. No. 7834348

The Memoirs Publishing Group supports both The Forest Stewardship Council® (FSC®) and the PEFC® leading international forest-certification organisations. Our books carrying both the FSC label and the PEFC® and are printed on FSC®-certified paper. FSC® is the only forest-certification scheme supported by the leading environmental organisations including Greenpeace. Our paper procurement policy can be found at www.memoirspublishing.com/environment

Typeset in 11/16pt Plantin
by Wiltshire Associates Publisher Services Ltd. Printed and bound in
Great Britain by Printondemand-Worldwide, Peterborough PE2 6XD

CONTENTS

The Imaginary Man	P. 1
Sleeping Beauty	P. 39
The Flirt	P. 78
As If!	P. 110
A Suspicious Mind	P. 145
I Wish	P. 174
Why me?	P. 210

I am good, but not an angel. I do sin, but I am not the devil. I am just a small girl in a big world trying to find someone to love.

Marilyn Monroe

THE IMAGINARY MAN

To be jilted at the altar once could be regarded as bad luck; twice is just plain careless. Such was the fate of my friend Eve. I'd been her bridesmaid at both her weddings, and both of them had gone horribly wrong. Whereas men seemed compelled to propose to her at the drop of a hat, they were less inclined to show up at church to go through with the ceremony. Twice so far, and counting, she'd been stood up.

The first time was truly awful, as I had nothing to compare it with. As we arrived at the church in our limos, the blushing bride was radiating beauty on her great day. The usher unexpectedly signalled for us to go round the block one more time.

'Why the hell's that?' screamed Eve.

'Oh, nothing to worry about. He's probably got his thing stuck in his zipper,' I said, trying to lighten the mood.

Trouble was, not only had his thing not made it to the church, neither had any other part of him. We did two more circuits in our sleek black cars in vain. I'd never seen so many tears or heard as much wailing as I did when Eve realised that her bridegroom had destroyed her marital dreams.

Of course I was sad for her, even though there was a tiny little part of me which had just about had it up to here with the smugness of soon-to-be-married people. And I'd also had to contend with her fiancée, who kept on giving me inappropriate looks and making improper suggestions whenever she was out of earshot.

Should I have told her of my suspicions prior to the service? Then she would think I was her frenemy, jealous of her success in getting a man to commit.

What kind of a guy could do something like that? Well, the same type of guy who stood her up on wedding day number two, only this one worried me even more. On the surface he was her romantic hero, always professing his love to her with poems and gifts.

'Isn't he a treasure?' she once said to me, when only twelve hours earlier he'd been sexting me saying how we should get it together while Eve was out of town on some business course. Of course, I replied, 'fuck off, and if you ever write or speak to me like that again I will expose you for the cheat you so obviously are.'

I don't think I'd ever led either of these men on, and in almost every respect Eve was so much prettier and more radiant than me – so what was I supposed to do? Always stay a hundred miles away from her latest fiancé, I guess.

'What's wrong with me? Eve wailed after number two had texted her on the morning of her next wedding that he couldn't go through with it.

'Nothing,' I said gently as I held her weeping in my arms. 'You're so pretty. What's not to like?'

'Pretty, but not sexy like you,' she replied, struggling to speak amid the tears.

'He's just a creep. It might not seem like it now, but you're so better off without him.'

'So you never liked Eddie then? Why didn't you tell me?' she railed at me. It was exactly what I was dreading. I certainly wasn't going to reveal his inappropriate message to me.

'You'll be telling me next that you never liked Alan either.' He was fiancé number one, in case you hadn't already guessed.

'Well, I wasn't exactly wild about him, but then I wasn't marrying the guy, was I?' I replied. Thankfully she had no answer to that.

And while I could get a little irritated by the lovey-doveyness of these clinging couples, I wasn't the kind of girl who was going to sleep with her best friend's fiancé – or should I say fiancés? As if I needed to steal my best friend's boyfriends. I was more than capable of attracting my own; trouble was, they weren't the type who wanted to take me up the aisle, at least in the wedding sense.

'I think men reckon your kind of dirty,' Eve once said to me in a less stressful, more drunken moment. 'Not the type most guys would ever consider taking home to Mom.'

'Whereas you're perfect daughter-in-law material,' I replied, giggling over the chardonnay.

'Only until the wedding day comes,' she said, wiping the intoxicated smile from my face.

Whatever unintended signals I was giving out to these men of Eve's I would smother them at source when it came to fiancé number three. I would dispense with make-up and slip on a burka, because I was willing to do absolutely anything not to distract this new guy Tom from showing up at church on time.

Of course, I did try to counsel Eve about rushing into another wedding after her previous disasters, but this one was different, or so she proclaimed. And for a short while I thought she might be right. He was more the strong silent type, a professional footballer who exuded old-fashioned masculine values. OK, so I might have been drawn to him had he not been betrothed to my best friend, and whatever little bit of envy I'd once betrayed about all the smugness of an engaged couple had now totally evaporated. All I totally wanted was to get my best friend married, so I could get on with my life as a self-employed beautician who ran her own salon, when not being pursued by single, unattached men who didn't want to commit.

So it came as something of a shock when Tom called in at my salon at the end of business – normally a no-go area for macho sporty guys, as you well know – declaring that he must speak to me, or else he would go mad.

'It's my shoulder,' he said. 'Can you manipulate while I talk?'

'No way,' I said, but I foolishly took him into a darkened room where mystic music played and sweet perfume permeated the air. Perhaps that's what set him off.

'So what's your problem?' I enquired as half-heartedly as I could.

'This wedding – I'm not sure I can go through with it. Unless you let me fuck you.'

I stepped back instinctively.

'I can't get you out of my head. And I know I shouldn't feel like this, only a few days before getting married.'

'Too right you shouldn't,' I replied. I put the top back on my bottle of cleansing oil. 'Consider me strictly forbidden.'

'Not that I want to marry you. You're just not that type.'

'You really know how to make a girl feel good, don't you?'

'I need to get you out of my system.'

'You do know that Eve is my life-long friend, and she has already been stood up by two other guys on her wedding day.'

'Precisely, and by having sex with me, you'll be guaranteeing she won't be making it three in a row.'

'So I'd be doing her a favour. How sick are you?'

'Come on, you know you want me,' he said. He slid his arm around my waist. The problem was, in spite of finding him one of the most despicable men on earth, as his lips touched mine for a brief moment I responded. That drove him on to lay me on the couch and lie on top of me. He was kissing me ever harder, while I let my lips part, allowing him to place his tongue in my mouth. I was disgusted by myself – how could I?

'This isn't going to happen,' I said, struggling to get off the couch. He pushed me back again.

'No fucking way,' I told him. 'You totally revolt me.'

'Yeah right,' he said, disbelieving, as I found the strength to set myself free.

'You get the hell out of here,' I commanded him. 'And don't think I won't be telling Eve about this.'

'Me too. I don't know what she's going to think when she hears how you lured me over to your salon to seduce me.'

'She'd never listen to you.'

'She already knows what type of girl you are. Let's see who she believes.'

Even in the heat of battle, I knew I couldn't risk it.

'Just give me a hand job and we'll call it quits,' he said.

'Do you know what, for one brief moment I actually found you sexually attractive, but I wouldn't have sex with you now even if you, Donald Trump and Hugh Hefner were the only men left alive on earth.'

That's how much I meant it.

So, it wasn't long before it became three no-shows in

succession. Perhaps he had a conscience after all, because how could Tom have possibly gone through with the wedding after everything he'd said to me? He could never have looked me in the face again, and that would have made my best friend suspicious. Better to leave Eve in the lurch than go through with what would have been a farce of a marriage.

Oh yes, and it totally got me off the hook too, as I'd been struggling to work out how I could possibly explain Tom's visit to the salon without Eve becoming convinced that I'd led him on. Either way I would have been screwed.

So, he stood her up at the altar too – not even a text to soften the blow – although this time I was totally relieved, however hard I tried to disguise it, whereas Eve unsurprisingly went into shock upon his non-arrival at the church.

Much more worrying than the tears and tantrums of her previous wedding day disasters was the eerie silence which greeted this latest catastrophe. In fact, not only did she fail to shed a tear, she simply stopped speaking, as if words were incapable of encapsulating how she felt.

Her parents called in the doctor the next day, and within twenty-four hours she'd been admitted to a nearby psychiatric unit, such was the trauma she'd been subjected to. Oh, how my heart went out to her! I was such a terrible thing to witness – your best friend locked away under sedation in a special medical unit. She couldn't have looked more forlorn.

I tried to raise her spirits by explaining that losing that

creep Tom would ultimately be the greatest blessing ever. I added that there were plenty of great guys out there, but she didn't have to marry them all.

She stared at me, speechless, with these big vacant eyes, as if she had taken a vow of silence, and would never speak again.

On the way out of her ward, after another one-sided conversation, I was approached by a nurse who asked whether I could spare a few minutes to talk to Eve's consultant psychiatrist. Of course I agreed, as I really wanted to know how long it would be before Eve talked again, and if there was anything I could do to get her speaking.

I guess I was expecting an old guy with glasses and a Sigmund Freud-style beard, not the über-hot young blonde in a tight-fitting white coat with critical curves in all the right places.

'Take a seat, Madison,' she said, giving me a conspiratorial wink. 'I would love to hear you talking about your friend Eve to see how we might be able to help her.'

'I would be only too happy to help, doctor.'

'Please – call me Ella.'

'Whatever I can do to help, Ella.'

I told her all about the three no-shows at three different wedding services, and how I had witnessed Eve's gradual decline after every disaster unfolded.

'And did any of these men give any hint that they might not be willing to go through with the ceremony in the run up to the wedding?' she asked.

'Kind of,' I said, feeling distinctly uncomfortable about going any further.

'I am I right in thinking that some of these men might have made sexual advances to you?'

I blushed. How long was it since I'd done that – Junior High?

'Well, if I'm honest, all of them – but I promise, I did nothing to encourage any of them,' I protested.

'I don't doubt it. You and I both know where we are coming from. There's a certain kind of woman who can't help but attract the attention of almost any kind of man, regardless of whether we give out signals or not.'

'Oh it's so great to talk to somebody who understands exactly what I have to deal with, because you've been there too. Do you mind me asking – are you married?'

'I wish,' she replied.

'I thought not. What is it about women like us that makes men feel we don't want commitment?'

'If I could answer that, I would have written a best-selling self-help book on it by now,' she said through a pained smile.

'But you really shouldn't blame yourself for her three failed weddings. The chances are your friend Eve simply keeps on picking the wrong type of man, the kind who thinks he's ready to commit, won over by her undoubted prettiness and sweet personality, until something else kicks in – his base animal desires. And if it hadn't been you who besotted him, then it could have been me, or some other woman who fitted the profile.'

I breathed an inward sigh of relief.

'But how can we restore her to her old self?'

'It will take time,' Ella warned me. 'Plus we'll have to eradicate her obsession about getting married, but we'll save that for another day. First, we need to bring her out of her self-imposed isolation, and to do that, we need to learn how to enter her world.'

I was listening intently, trying not to become transfixed by Ella's bosom. And I'm not at all gay, in case that's what you're thinking.

She smiled, her body swinging around towards mine on her swivel chair.

'So how do we enter Eve's world?' I enquired, endeavouring to concentrate on the matter in question.

'Try not to argue or disagree with her if she starts coming out with strange views or opinions. Treat everything she says as the gospel truth, as if it had been sworn on the Bible in a court of law. Strive to believe in everything she says, however weird it might seem, until she is able to distinguish between reality and fantasy of her own accord, and only then can we progress to the next stage.'

'That's most helpful,' I said. 'Thank you for your understanding and guidance.'

I couldn't help but notice that Ella had luscious lips. Most men would be powerless to resist her.

It was only after my third visit to see Eve in the Unit that she started to speak. It began with nothing much more than the occasional yes or no, then started building towards some basic stuff about how she'd been sleeping, the quality of the food, and how coffee always smelt better than it tasted.

As the early spring weather softened we started to take strolls in the hospital grounds, talking as we walked, although never mentioning what had happened at the church. It was as if she had erased those dreadful events from her mind. Ella explained it was Eve's way of coping, and to be encouraged for the moment.

'Sometimes a small amount of denial is good for us,' said Ella at one of our regular chats.

It wasn't long before we decided that it would be beneficial for Eve to go home. Ella congratulated me on the important role I had played in helping to restore Eve to something approaching full mental health, and then asked if I would be willing to continue reporting back to her.

Of course, I was only too happy to say yes. Not only did I appreciate how much it was benefiting Eve, I was learning things about myself too which were wondrous to reflect upon.

Once back home with her Mom and Dad, Eve quickly began picking up the threads of her old life, without a wedding proposal in sight. We would go down town together for a little therapeutic shopping, followed by girly chats in our favourite Italian restaurant about what our preferred film stars were up to and who they were dating. And somehow that led to us talking about taking a trip to Europe, and before we had even reached the tiramisu we were scribbling down our agenda for our forthcoming European tour.

So what could be normal than that? I was only too pleased to recount it to Ella at our next meeting at the unit. However, Ella felt otherwise.

'She's suppressing her true feelings by focusing on other stuff, but sooner or later, it will all come bursting out,' she said. 'She needs to confront what's happened to her, otherwise I fear for her long-term mental future.'

What was I supposed to do? Plus, I don't mind admitting that this whole business of reporting back to Ella was beginning to make me feel a touch uncomfortable, as if I was in some way betraying Eve by acting as her doctor's go-between.

And was it just me, or was Ella displaying a little more cleavage every time I visited her? Her body language seemed to accentuate her formidable bosom, and she seemed to be leaning in my direction at every opportunity.

'Well if you'd rather we stopped meeting like this… I'm sure it can't be easy for you, being girlie in the middle,' she said, as if she'd been reading my mind.

'No, I think we should carry on,' I replied. I was feeling almost powerless to resist, although common sense told me that I should really bring these meetings to a close.

'Have you ever heard that expression, 'let sleeping dogs lie?' I dared to ask Ella, who all too easily understood the implication of my question.

'Trouble is, sleeping dogs eventually wake up and start barking, and Eve's dogs are no exception to the rule.'

So I reluctantly demurred.

'Expect the unexpected,' she went on. 'Just when Eve appears to have returned to normal she will probably do something alarming and irrational, so you'll have to be prepared. You're my eyes and ears. Let's meet up again in another two weeks.'

Was more therapy really what Eve needed? A couple of encounters of the sexual kind on our forthcoming European tour with some hot Italian or French guys would do her better than a bunch of sessions with Ella. Unless Eve went loopy on me within the next few days I was going to assume that my best friend was well on the road to recovery and formally resign as Ella's little helper.

I wasn't that worried when Eve first started telling me about this incredible guy she'd met, although I have to admit that my heart did start to sink a little when she mentioned the dreaded W word in passing.

'Please don't tell me he wants to marry you?' I asked, daring to mention the subject which cannot speak its name.

'Well, yes he does, but I told him not to be so ridiculous to even think of such a thing after only one meeting.'

So that reassured me about Eve's soundness of mind, although what kind of guy proposes marriage during a first date? The kind who climbs in through your bedroom window at two in the morning apparently, which is exactly what happened, if Eve was to be believed.

'Did you call the police to arrest him for breaking and entering?'

'No, why should I? He was doing it because he loved me, and since when has love become a federal offence?'

Expect the unexpected – that's what Ella had warned me. Humour her – try getting into how her mind works.

'And what was he called, this midnight caller?'

'It was well after two, and his name was Aragorn, Prince of Passion.'

'I see,' I said, trying not to laugh.

'Do I detect the merest hint of incredulity on your face?' Eve pushed me.

'No, not at all. What did you talk about?'

'We talked of forests, and glades, and hillsides where he hunted with his sword, brandishing it in the cause of justice against those who would smite the people.'

How could I be expected to play along with this nonsense? I seemed to remember fiancé number two being a Lord of the Rings obsessive – maybe some of that had rubbed off on her.

'And did it go any further than talking?'

'Trust you to bring up sex,' she admonished me, 'but it would have been hard not to. I tell you Madison, I came so close to giving out on a first date.'

'That's if you can call a guy climbing through your window at three o'clock in the morning a date.'

'It was two o'clock, actually. Why do I get the feeling you're not taking this seriously?'

'Oh I so am,' I said remembering Ella's advice about

getting inside her head. 'So let's get down to the real nitty gritty – hot or not?'

'Hot! He's the most amazing man ever created, and virtually impossible to resist. You wouldn't have tried too hard to fight him off.'

'So that's what you think of me.'

'He had the blackest of jet black hair, the brownest of eyes, the most sensuous of smiles, the strongest of arms, the pertest of bottoms, the longest of…'

'Whooo!'

'I was going to say, legs, plus the most manipulative of hands, the deepest of voices…'

'He sounds fucking gorgeous,' I said, forgetting for a moment that we were talking about a figment of her imagination.

'Would you like to meet him?'

'Do you know, I'm not sure whether that's such a good idea.'

'Why ever not?'

'It's not like it's gone that well in the past with your previous boyfriends, plus won't he be too busy smiting in the forests?'

'What do you think I am, some kind of lunatic? Of course he gets time off from his job with the Forestry Commission in New Hampshire. He'll be staying over next weekend- we'll go for lunch. I'll see you there at Luigi's – I'll book a table for three.'

That was as sane a thing as I'd heard so far, had it not been that this perfect guy had allegedly climbed through her window in the dead of the night to propose marriage to her.

I seriously needed to speak to Ella, so I rushed down to the hospital without an appointment, but I couldn't find her anywhere.

'I think she may have gone,' one of the nurses advised me. But then I stumbled into the ladies' rest room to see Ella taking off her white doctor's coat to reveal only a bra and panties protecting her modesty – and believe me, she had nothing to be modest about.

'Eve, how lovely to see you! What can I do for you?' she said smiling from ear to ear, completely unconcerned about her semi-clothed state. She seemed to enjoy my embarrassment.

'Er… ah…' I gasped. I was still out of breath from running all the way there.

'It's not disturbing you Eve, seeing me like this? she said, referring to her provocative underwear. 'It's a good job the patients and their families don't realise what I wear next to my doctor's coat.' She laughed lasciviously. 'It's just more comfortable this way.'

'Of course,' I said, my eyes nearly popping out of my head.

'Eve… you're not just a little bit lesbian, are you?'

'No, not at all!'

'Ah. Simply bi-curious then?'

'Not in the least. I'm strictly for guys, and plenty of them,' I said, trying much too hard to be convincing.

'Shame, because the most recent medical research

conclusively proves that almost every woman has gay desires, although whether they choose to act upon them is another matter.'

'But it's not about me. I desperately need to talk to you about Eve. She's completely lost the plot.' While Ella nonchalantly slipped into a bodice and black evening dress, I started blurting out Eve's astonishing admission about her fantasy love life.

'Calm down,' said Ella, placing the back of her hand on my forehead, then feeling my pulse. 'You're in such a state. I fear this might be all too much for you. Sit down.' She gestured for me to relax with a gentle flow of her arm. 'Try one of these.' She handed me a strip of silver foil containing some little red pills, and poured out a glass of water to help me gulp me one down. 'And it if it ever gets too much for you again, just take one or two of these again.'

I should have asked her what the hell I'd just swallowed, but whenever I was with Ella all sense seemed to go out of the window – and this was the woman who'd been charged with making Eve well again. Only trouble was, I was getting ill in the process.

'If you think you're up to it, I want you to meet this Aragorn,' she went on. 'He almost certainly doesn't exist, but you'll have to pretend like crazy that he's actually there. And those pills should help relax you – I would strongly advise you take a couple just before you go out to meet her – or should I say, them.'

I felt a little woozy as I got up to go. I was swaying

unsteadily, feeling both light-headed and light-hearted, as I fell into Eva's arms.

'Shall we dance?' I quipped.

'If you like,' she replied. 'Who's going to lead?'

'Oh, you are so going to lead. You're definitely in charge,' I replied. 'And where are you going tonight?'

'I'm being taken out to dinner by a senior consultant in gynaecology, allegedly to talk about his ground-breaking new paper on female arousal. Nothing beats a man who knows his way around.'

'Oh god, I do like you!' I said joining in her laughter.

'I'm getting you a taxi,' she said moving me towards a chair. She booked me a ride back to my apartment before she sped off into the night for what I assumed would be another evening of earth-moving, ground-braking, but ultimately meaningless, sex with a powerful, handsome man.

Our dinner at Luigi's with Eve and her whatever was set for the following lunch time. I saw no point in dragging this nonsense out – I wasn't designed to be an undercover psychotherapist, I was a beautician with my own salon, and while I had listened to plenty of hair-raising stories from clients about their sexual exploits while doing a Brazilian, I hadn't been trained to counsel somebody as seriously deluded as Eve.

I walked into Luigi's to see Eve sitting at the table with not one but two empty, waiting chairs. I kissed Eve in our usual air-kissy kind of way and then I took a deep breath and smiled at the empty chair.

'Aragorn, how lovely to make your acquaintance, I've heard so much about you,' I said, holding out my hand to his imaginary hand shake.

'Madison? What the hell is wrong with you? Aragorn is away in the rest room. Are you all right?'

So who was the crazy one around here? Sorting out Eve's fantasies was clearly sending me insane. Isn't that what happens to some psychiatrists? I've heard they often finish up madder than their patients.

'He's not feeling so hungry, so he'll only be joining us for a drink,' Eve explained.

'Well that explains everything,' I replied.

'Ah, here he is. Aragorn, meet Madison.'

And still I was staring at nothing.

Could this be another of her tricks, designed to make me question my sanity – or should I follow Ella's advice and enthusiastically join her world?

'Good to meet you,' I said with as much enthusiasm as I could manage,' I said. This time I tried air-kissing her imaginary man. An imaginary kiss for an imaginary person.

'He's thrilled to meet you,' Eve translated on his behalf.

'Not too thrilled, I hope.'

'Oh yes, as you can see, Aragorn, my friend Madison has this unfortunate habit of enticing men – she's that type of girl. Not that I'm suggesting she does anything to encourage it.'

I gave Eve a stare loaded with mixed emotions.

'He says, he's charmed, I'm sure,' Eve continued translating.

Now what?

'Aragorn says he doesn't want to get in the way of our girlie conversation, as he knows we've got a European tour to discuss.'

So we effectively ignored him for the next twenty minutes, which was a relief for all concerned, although Aragorn would occasionally interrupt with some observation about the dangers of being robbed in Rome, or the high cost of gas in England, as voiced by Eve.

Hell, was I glad to know that Aragorn approved of our itinerary. So much so that I retreated to the ladies' restroom to try and restore my sanity. I had endured this fiasco for longer than I cared. How was I going to survive another half an hour of this? I could either drink more wine, get hopelessly drunk and start insulting Aragorn with such phrases as 'I can see right through you' or I could take one, or maybe two, of Ella's potent pills. I decided on the drug option. Well, she was a doctor after all, and she'd recommended that it might help get me through the experience of dining with a slightly warped friend and her invisible boyfriend.

They had an almost immediate effect, both lifting my spirits and making me feel more connected with those parts of the world which bemused me, like non-existent boyfriends. And as I freshened up in the bathroom I began recalling Eve's incredible description of this man. It had sounded so vivid I'd felt a frisson of desire.

So perhaps that was the way to go; imagine your own ideal man, and he will come. And while I was considering Aragorn's alleged assets, I would add an impressive six-pack, an eye-catching bulge and a love of listening. I would also banish bad morning breath, farting in bed and scratching his own balls – not too much to ask for, was it?

Apparently not, because upon my return there was a man sitting at the table; a real one. In fact, he was my version of Aragorn, exactly as I had imagined him – as far as I could see, that is, given that he was fully (and very well) dressed. He was sitting nonchalantly at the table. He looked enlivened by my reappearance and greeted me ardently, which must have been duly noted by Eve.

'You're here,' was all I could manage in reply. How come I wasn't talking to an empty space any more?

'What a strange thing to say,' said Eve. 'Where did you think he would be? Aragorn wouldn't have left without saying goodbye. I reckon he's got the hots for you!'

'Eve, please.'

'You see Aragorn, most of my gentleman friends can't take their eyes off Eve. Once seen, never forgotten, and it seems you're no different from all of the others.'

'But they only ever want to marry you,' I said without thinking.

'Thanks so much for opening that particular can of worms,' she said. She grabbed her hand bag, shot to her feet and flounced off to the rest room.

'Oh God, what have I done? I wasn't thinking properly,' I said to Aragorn, who was looking on with a mixture of amusement and alarm.

'You shouldn't beat yourself up,' he said.

'It's these pills I've been taking. They send me a little crazy.'

'I kind of like crazy,' he replied.

I had to stop myself for a moment. Here I was talking to a man who only minutes ago had appeared not to exist. In fact I was opening up my heart to him, and getting a little turned on in the process.

'Do you? Well that's me, I guess. It's my meds you see.'

'I can see why Eve's boyfriends get a little distracted by you' he replied. 'She said something earlier about keeping you out of sight.'

'That's just Eve's style of humour. But then she does have this dumb idea that I'm catnip for men.'

'Meow,' he replied, which kind of got me purring.

So far I'd hardly put a foot wrong when it came to being loyal and supportive to my best friend. But boy, was she pushing her luck with her insults and increasingly erratic behaviour. It was enough to drive a girl mad. And boy, was I finding it hard not to flirt with the extraordinarily handsome Aragorn. After all, what the hell – he didn't really exist, did he?

'I think we should we meet up later to discuss Eve – just you and me,' he said. He handed me a card with his hotel room number written on it.

'Are you for real?'

'You'll have to call round if you want to find out.'

At that point Eve's reappearance brought that particular avenue of conversation to a dead end. 'You seem to be getting on really well,' she giggled nervously.

I smiled a forced smile, while Aragon looked on impassively.

'And I know you didn't mean any harm, Madison, by your unfortunate comment. We're not going to let your thoughtlessness ruin a great lunch.'

I could have slapped her face. After everything I'd tried to do for her in the wake of all her wedding disasters to coax her back to something approaching a normal life, although there was clearly a long way to go.

'I do hope we can meet up again soon,' said Aragorn. His quick intervention stopped me from saying something I might have regretted.

'Oh real soon,' I said. He kissed me on both cheeks. I loved the smell of him, the feel of him, the force of him.

'Well, what do you think?' Eve excitedly asked me after Aragorn had departed.

'He's all right, if you're into fantasy novels. He's straight out of the *Lord of the Rings*, like his name.'

'Obviously. So you approve?'

'What's not to like, except that ridiculous name?'

'Call him whatever you like. He's strange like that.'

'Are you're seeing him again soon?'

'Next time he's in town, for another one of his business conferences.'

'Well, why wouldn't you?' I said, appearing to be disinterested.

'I can sense your pain, Madison,' said Eve. She was nauseatingly holding my hand. 'But one day soon, you're going to meet somebody special too. OK, he might not be as breathtakingly amazing as Aragorn, because we can't all be so lucky in love as I've become, can we?'

I smiled ever more weakly at her, like my face was running low on happiness gas. We air-kissed one another goodbye, with a noticeable lack of sincerity on my part. The dumb expression of caring concern on hers made me even more determined that my next port of call would be Room 408 at the Holiday Inn, Boston, Bunker Hill. Only to find out more about him, you understand, and to try and evaluate where he stood in relation to my friend. If there was any uncertainty about his intentions – which could be the case, since he'd just handed me his room number – I would send him on his way. Oh yes, and did he really exist?

I took another of Ella's pills to give me even more medically-induced courage. Now I would feel invincible. And no sooner had I walked into the hotel lobby than I dived into the ladies' rest room to wait for the pills to really kick in, and apply a little extra lipstick and mascara. Not that I wanted him to find me attractive in any sense whatsoever – it was all about giving me confidence to do what a woman had to do.

Maybe I should have called him on the hotel lobby phone and arranged to meet him in the entrance hall, but instead I marched straight up to his room, took three deep breaths and knocked vigorously on his door.

He'd obviously just stepped out of the shower, judging by the way he was dressed. All he had on was a towel tied around his waist.

'I was expecting you,' he said.

'Well, you could have dressed for it,' I replied.

'I have,' he said.

That should have been the cue for me to wave him goodbye, but of course I accepted his invitation to join him for a drink. God, he was so ripped. His smooth chest was glistening with droplets of water trickling inevitably south. I'd only encountered a truly irresistible man twice before in my life, and this was most definitely occasion number three, and by far the best yet. How I didn't rip the towel from his waist I will never know. I guess I was still driven by the urge to ensure that he wasn't leading my best friend a merry dance. She would never survive another breakdown.

'What is the meaning of all this, Aragorn?' I said accusingly.

'Ice? He enquired as he fixed me a vodka and tonic. He took a place right next to me on the sofa, making me feel uncomfortably close.

'What are you playing at with my friend Eve?' I asked him. 'She has all sorts of crazy ideas about you. She claimed that you asked her to marry you, after only one date.'

'So what if I did?'

'You know she's been stood up at the altar on three separate occasions? And what's this about climbing through her bedroom window?'

'She must have been speaking figuratively,' he claimed, as I took a sip of my drink.

'Meaning?'

'That I arrived unexpectedly in her life. But the way she spoke to you today – nobody should ever address a friend like that.'

'Perhaps that's what friends are for – people who will let you say absolutely anything, and then forgive them for it,' I said. 'So why have you invited me to your room?'

'To talk about Eve? And I could ask you the same question back.'

'I'm concerned for Eve too, that's all.'

'I think we both know that neither of us is telling the complete truth.'

I reflected on that for a moment. Then I turned to him and looked him straight in the eye. I could feel the blood rushing to my lips, my nipples tingling with excitement, my pussy craving him, but I wasn't going to submit… except that I'd never felt like this about a man before.

'Only if it's a meaningless one-off, and won't in any way affect your continued relationship with Eve,' I said as I traced my finger along the centre of his extravagantly manly chest. So shocking. So wrong.

'Strictly a one-afternoon stand,' he confirmed as I further explored his heavenly torso.

'The story of my life,' I said, laughing. I was remembering that I hadn't had sex for a good while – or maybe it was some kind of revenge against Eve, who had succeeded in really getting under my skin. 'For me to even think of betraying my friend like this, you'd better be worth it.' Then I shamelessly whipped away the white towel from his waist. 'Oh boy, you're worth it,' I said, looking at what I had revealed.

First he kissed me teasingly, and then passionately, on the lips. I was swooning – I'm not sure I'd ever swooned before.

'Size queen eh?' he said.

'Modest eh?' I replied. Then I went down on him.

Unlike some well-blessed guys I'd previously encountered, he wasn't a lazy lover. His tongue produced shock waves of pleasure inside me, like little earthquakes shaking me to the core. I'll be honest with you, I haven't always been that relaxed about men going down on me; sometimes I find it difficult to abandon myself, feeling uncomfortable about the lack of control. But with Aragorn, I was at one with him and my own sexuality, happy to surrender to his ingenious mouth.

And then he entered me – and when I say 'entered', that harmless little word could hardly do it justice. How could I not shout about it? It was more like the introduction of the great gladiator Spartacus into the Colosseum, worthy of spectators, and musicians and fireworks too. Call the pleasure police, there's a woman having too much fun in there. Who cared if we got arrested?

I lost count of the number of orgasms, as that song *Man, I Feel Like a Woman* went through my head. I started singing it out loud without realising – how totally embarrassing was that?

'I've made plenty of women scream, but I've never

made a woman sing before,' he said as I climbed on top of him and began to serenade him Shania Twain-style.

In brief, we had a really great time. We carried on making out for most of the afternoon, until finally I retreated to the bathroom to take a shower. I was kind of hoping he would join me for a gently sensual conclusion to our astonishing lovemaking, but he didn't show.

And then I heard a female voice asking, was there anybody in there? That confused me no end. I got out the shower and draped myself in one of those white bathrobes you only ever see in five-star hotels. Upon re-entering the main suite, there was no sign of Aragorn. Instead I was confronted by a worried looking Filipina maid.

'I think you must be in the wrong room,' the maid said.

Of course she was right, but I couldn't admit it.

'Come on, we're all grown-ups here. I'm a friend of Mr Aragorn Prince, and this is his room.'

She examined her chart with a bewildered frown. 'No, this room is definitely empty. It's out of commission because of an unfortunate stain on the carpet.' She pointed to the spot where I had earlier been making love with that gorgeous man. There was no evidence of his clothes or belongings, just my unfinished vodka and tonic and my clothes and underwear scattered around the room.

I had only one thing on my mind – escape. Fearing she might call senior management at any moment, I retreated back to the bathroom to get dressed in one heck of a hurry, and then handed her a generous tip in return for her silence, which she gratefully accepted.

That bastard of a man had only gone and walked out on me. What a horribly insensitive way to finish our afternoon of physical delight.

And then a cold shiver started to run down my spine. Had he even been there at all? Was I suffering delusions about having hot sex with unbelievably gorgeous men in hotel rooms, and if so why? What the hell was happening to me?

And then I had a brainwave. I knew who to ask – my psychiatrist friend Ella, who had an answer to everything. Maybe it was something to do with those pills I had taken, as prescribed by her.

As I traveled home on the T Line I had to kick myself mentally for daring to doubt what had happened between me and Aragorn in the hotel room. But I would speak to Ella anyway. Perhaps I should finally quit my role as go-between between Ella and Eve – it was obviously getting to me.

First I popped round to see my parents, to pour out my heart to my mom about the strain Eve was putting me through.

'She was a good friend to you when you were going through your wild stage,' she said. 'I guess now it's your turn to return the compliment.'

I only half agreed with her – and what did she mean by my wild stage? That was simply growing up, wasn't it?

'But I want you to know that your dad and I will always stick by you, even if it might not seem like it when it happens.'

I couldn't begin to think what she meant by that. My mom did have this rather annoying habit of speaking in riddles, so I didn't really give it any significance at the time.

I would have called in to see Eve too, but I just couldn't face her after what had seemingly passed between Aragorn and me, unless I'd imagined the whole thing. So I checked in with Ella the next day at the hospital, and she was looking especially vivacious, as if she'd been having great sex with her tame gynaecologist.

'Come in,' she said, waving me into her office and then shutting the door. Then she started unbuttoning her white coat, to reveal a stunning Chantilly lace strappy bustier.

'You like?' she said.

'Wow!' I cried out loud.

'My date bought me this – surprisingly good taste for a man, don't you think?' She gave me a wink. 'So I made him promise to wear my red satin knickers under his boring grey suit at his next consultation in return. If only his patients knew.'

'They might think he was taking all that being in touch with your feminine side a bit far,' I joked, not really wanting to waste time on her sex life – mine was so much more extraordinary.

'And he gave me this beautiful dress too,' she said holding up a stunning red gown. 'And you're welcome to borrow it. It will be such fun to swap clothes when you finally move in.'

I couldn't fathom what she was going on about, so I insisted on telling her about Eve's imaginary man, and how I'd been obliged to talk to a non-existent character, not to mention how weird it had made me feel.

'Did you try taking the pills?' she asked me.

'Yes, and it really helped. Within minutes I could see what she saw.'

'Which was?'

'A highly attractive man, although I'm not sure if my version wasn't slightly different from Eve's version, strange as that might seem.'

'Well, it's not exactly what you would call normal behaviour, is it?' That was the first hint that not everything was as it should be. 'And did he respond to you? Sorry, silly question – of course he did. All men, whether real or imaginary, are touched by your presence.'

'That's been greatly over-exaggerated by Eve' I protested. She's got this thing about my supposed ability to attract men.'

'And from where I'm sitting, she might just be right,' said Ella, flicking her hair as she spoke.

I waved my arm dismissively.

'So you actually talked to what you now consider to have been a real man?'

'I did. It must have been the pills.'

'They aren't that strong.'

'And then while Eve was away in the restroom, he asked me to visit him at his hotel.'

'I see. And did you?'

'Look, I know it was wrong… and I never went there with the intention of fucking him.'

'You say you had sex with this guy who doesn't even exist.'

'The best ever. He would have put your gynaecologist to shame.'

'Except my man was real, unless I was seriously mistaken by that big bold cock which was forever going in and out of me.'

'That's just how it was for me.'

'Madison, sweetheart, I've already been in touch with your parents about the best form of treatment for you, and they are willing to fund it, indefinitely.'

'I beg your pardon?'

'We both agree that you would benefit from spending a little time with us.'

'I'm not the crazy one! That's my friend Eve, unless you've forgotten.'

'That's what we all thought at first, my sweet thing, until I began to piece together the jigsaw that made up the dynamic of your fractured relationship. That's when I realised that it was you who needed help. Eve is as sane as I am.'

'I refuse to listen to any more of this!' I said, getting up to go.

'I'm afraid you can't leave. I won't let you. But if you insist on it, I will be forced to invoke a court order, already signed by your parents, which compels you to stay here for as long as I see fit. It's for your own good.'

I looked at her in utter disbelief, all words failing me.

'What's not to like? Just think of all the girlie fun we can have together. We can talk about men, and clothes, and make-up, and maybe we can even practice French kissing on one another, if you fancy – and I rather think you do.'

I wanted to say *you're sick*, but nothing came out.

'Oh dear, you have only gone and lost the power of speech. It's quite common in people who've been experiencing intolerable stress. It will come back, but only after a very long time.'

I could only rock backwards and forwards in the manner of a child showing its disapproval while trying to comfort itself at the same time.

'You'll be my pretty little pet,' she said. 'Besides, I've already agreed with Eve's family that you'll be kept under lock and key until she has married her latest fiancé. We don't want you sabotaging any more of her weddings, do we?'

She had robbed me of who I was, and sickeningly, I could sense myself succumbing to her will.

'Always the bridesmaid, never the bride,' she said, escorting me along a never-ending corridor towards what was about to become my new home. 'Do make yourself comfortable.' She opened the door and ushered me into a small, square room. 'I've already explained to your parents that this type of therapy can take anything between eight and ten years to achieve results.'

I was beyond afraid.

'Honey, I can really sense your fear,' she said as she held me against her ample bosom. 'I'm not just doing this for me. I'm doing it for you too. Come on, don't fight it, let me kiss it better.' Her lips touched mine, and I was far too afraid to resist – or maybe I didn't want to. I had always found Ella attractive, and never more so now, as I placed my hand upon her breast.

'That's better, but only when you're truly ready. First, I've got somebody who would like to meet you again, and I'm sure you'll feel exactly the same about him."

Out of the shadows stepped Aragorn, looking more stunningly wonderful than even I could remember him.

'Only if you want to,' Ella assured me.

Well she cared for me, didn't she, and surely she must have my best interests at heart? And it was wonderful, even better than before. I got the feeling Ella might have been filming us, but it didn't constrain our lovemaking in any sense whatsoever.

He would come to my room almost every night, pretty much whenever I wanted him to be there, while during the day Ella would devote her time to me by carrying out interviews which explored my feelings both towards her and Aragorn. According to her initial analysis it seemed I pretty much liked them equally, although she was confident that it wouldn't be too long before I learned to love her more.

I was beginning to speak the odd word again too. I was practicing alone when along came a knock on the door.

'I've got a visitor for you,' said Ella. She was wearing

her hair up, which I really liked, because she had such adorable little ears.

The visitor was Eve.

'Don't get up,' she said. 'I've bought my wedding album to show you.'

'Isn't that great?' said Ella. 'I'll leave you two together.'

'Always the bridesmaid, never the bride, and now not even the bridesmaid,' she sneered as I identified the woman who had taken my place. It was Ella.

'But I forgive you for what you did with my other fiancés, now that Ella has explained how you couldn't help yourself – because you're sick, aren't you?'

I stared at her impassively. And it got freakier.

'So here's my husband,' she said with a chest full of pride. It was Aragorn who was pictured there, fulfilling his promise to marry her. 'Gorgeous, isn't he? But you'll never get your hands on him, because they're going to keep you in here forever.'

I was beginning to reflect that I didn't really like my friend so much anymore. Maybe that's why I suddenly recovered the power of speech.

'But that's where your wrong,' I said. 'I had your husband in the hotel after we had lunch together, and we've being seeing each other ever since.'

'You bitch. So just like all the others then.'

'No way. I only ever had Aragorn. He fucked me, ravished me, and I'm glad of it, because you pushed me too far.'

'You're totally delusional. Ella warned me what to

expect. Do you think Aragorn would ever betray me for you? In your dreams. And as for the others, you're welcome to them.' She flounced out of my room, all rolling eyes and huffing and puffing.

'Good riddance!' I shouted after her.

Clearly I was on the road to recovery, although it seemed nobody else quite saw it quite like that, now that the so-called sane had gone totally insane, while the likes of me were locked up behind bars. Never had that phrase 'the world's gone mad' felt more appropriate.

After several weeks of reflection, punctuated by numerous sessions with Ella, I began to get a grip on things, and a plan began to form in my mind. Much as I adored my nights with the Prince, I knew what I had to do. And I would announce it to Ella at our next therapy session, as it concerned her above all.

When the time came, she listened to my rather hostile account of my meeting with Eve, then responded by admonishing me for my negativity towards my former friend.

'Is it any wonder that she despairs of you after what happened with all those future husbands of hers?' she said accusingly. 'You must learn to take responsibility for your actions and respect boundaries.'

'Don't you love me anymore?' I said. I was crestfallen, but still determined to pursue my plan.

'Sometimes the truth hurts, Madison.'

'In that case,' I said, getting down on to one knee, 'Ella, will you marry me?'

She held out the palm of her hand directly to my face, and sighed deeply.

'After everything we've just discussed you go and ask me that,' she replied. I dropped my head in sorrow. 'How on earth am I supposed to answer, except by saying – of course I will, you silly girl. Why wouldn't I?'

'I'm truly blessed,' I replied.

'You may kiss the bride,' she said, a little prematurely.

I was happy to oblige, and we kissed one another lasciviously on the lips. Our passion was threatening to simmer over into something more full on.

'Stop! I want us to save ourselves for our wedding night – old fashioned I know,' said Ella drawing breath.

'If that's what you want,' I said.

'We'll have to keep our engagement secret whatever happens. Otherwise I could lose my job and you'd be transferred to another facility.'

'But love conquers all,' I proclaimed.

'Even love has its limits,' she replied. 'You'd better prepare yourself for a long engagement, because we won't be allowed to marry until you're out of here.'

'No problem, that will give me plenty of time to prepare our ceremony. You can leave all the planning to me.'

'That's a relief,' she said.

'First I need to get hold of the Victoria's Secret catalogue so I can order our lingerie – so important to get that right, don't you think? And then I'll design our wedding dresses, you in red and me in white.'

'I would have thought the colors should be other way around,' she argued. 'Oh, look at the time, our session has overrun. Anyhow we have achieved some really good work together this session, don't you think?'

That was probably the least romantic reaction to a wedding proposal ever. What a professional!

So that's about it really. You see, I suppose I ought to let you guys back at the salon know what's been going down. You must have been wondering where the hell I've been, not having heard from me in ages. So, please look upon this as your wedding invitation. I'm not quite sure of the date, or even the time and the place, as everything depends on what Ella has in mind. I suggest you clear a place in your diary for some time during the next ten years. Cancel all of the appointments at the salon if you like. It's likely to be a Saturday, if that's any help.

See you all there – I'll be the one who looks like a meringue.

RSVP Valley Stream Private Mental Health Facility.

SLEEPING BEAUTY

When people ask how we first met, I usually make some lame excuse and try to change the subject to absolutely anything else. Embarrassing doesn't do it when I'm trying to explain what really brought us together.

So let me tell you all about it.

You've probably heard of an American in Paris. Well, I was an American in Wolverhampton – much less glamorous, as the phrase suggests, because this unloved post-industrial English city had a reputation for being a little drab, and not the kind of place you would cross the Atlantic Ocean for. Yet I'd wanted to live in England ever since I had first read *Jane Eyre*, inspired by my love of all the great English writers of the eighteenth and nineteenth centuries, and the hope that I too might be swept off my feet in the manner of a romantic heroine by the perfect English gentleman.

All the time I was growing up in Atlanta, Georgia, I'd had these dreams of one day living in a cute little thatched cottage with roses growing around the front door. While I was sipping tea in the parlor I would wait for a handsome Hugh Grant lookalike to call to escort me to a Royal Garden Party, where I would turn Prince Harry's head, and make him mine, much to the distress of the Hugh Grant clone.

Unsurprisingly, it didn't quite work out like my dream. No sooner had I disembarked at Terminal Four Heathrow than I quickly found London to be far too pricey for a girl of my limited means – well, until I enlisted the help of the two Arab gentlemen who kindly offered to set me up in a Knightsbridge penthouse for their own personal pleasure. They must have noticed that I had the body of an uptown hooker. Unfortunately for them, I also had the mind of somebody who had a degree in philosophy and wasn't about to succumb to the whims of rich guys – Arab or otherwise – unless it was Omar Sharif in his prime. I just loved that old *Doctor Zhivago* movie.

Not that I'd ever been in the film business, but I had spent a few months working as an intern on WSB Atlanta News/Talk Radio, filling in between the ultra-opinionated commentators to deliver a few sweet nothings, followed by reports of the latest traffic snarl-ups. I'd planned on getting signed up by a top British radio franchise – who knows, even the BBC, hoping they might mistakenly think I was

Howard Stern in drag, and famous the length and breadth of the USA.

So it was something of a shock to the system when they didn't all come knocking on my door. Even to have received a letter of rejection would have been something.

That was until I got a belated response from an outfit in Wolverhampton. No, I hadn't heard of it either – and if I had known better, I probably wouldn't have set foot in the place, which would have been a big mistake, as the local people more than made up with their warmth and friendliness for the uninspiring landscape, which I eventually grew to love. And what's not to love about a pint of Banks's and a packet of pork scratchings on a Saturday night? Hey, too much geography, I hear you cry.

Did I ever fulfil my dream of ensnaring a true English gentleman? I wish. Instead I encountered a ghastly cavalcade of drunken oafs – what is it with the English and drink? – or at the other end of the spectrum, a couple of uptight upper-class idiots who ran the gamut of emotions all the way from A to B.

That was until I had an audience with Stan the Man, Radio Wolfie's numero uno disc jockey, who had so much get up and go that he might have invented the concept of high energy, had it not already been first discovered by Jim Carrey in *The Mask*. I first encountered this human whirlwind of a man when I was asked to contribute traffic reports to Stan the Man's lunch time show, where he teased me mercilessly about everything American, especially my choice of words – sidewalk instead of pavement, hood for bonnet and beltway instead of ring road.

'I'm having to learn a whole new language here,' I said, after he'd corrected me live again on air.

'That's because you're in a foreign country. Welcome to Englandville. It's so lovely to have you in our green and pleasant land, Miss America. And please don't go rabbiting on about your fanny. It means something different here!'

I thought this young guy was hilarious. He had so much exuberance, and that winning smile was warm enough to captivate even the coldest of hearts. In short, he had charisma plus. He took me under his professional wing, building up my 'part' as he called it, until I was almost co-hosting the show, although he stayed very much in charge. We developed this mock confrontational style with me as his female foil, plus plenty of transatlantic banter, which the listeners seemed to lap up. He appeared to be generous, brash, and probably a touch American, which was probably what drew me towards him, as maybe I was feeling a little lonely in a foreign land.

True, although he was four years older than me he could act a little immaturely at times, but I would encourage him to grow up without suffocating his charm, wouldn't I?

It didn't take long for our listeners to suspect that there was something going on between us long after our show had finished.

We had this well-rehearsed on air routine, which went something like this, and we pretty much did it every day.

'It's 12.28, and here's our very own traffic girl – the USA's loss is our gain. What have you got for me, Caro?'

'I've got hold ups on the M6, road works on the A453 and road closures around Cannock.'

'Get out of here!'

'OK.'

'Oh, and Caro…'

'Yes?'

'Will you marry me?'

'In your dreams, Stan.'

Except on this one particular day, instead of telling him to get lost, I unaccountably said, 'Why not?'

'Did she just say what I thought she said?' said Stan.

'She so did,' said the Station Producer on talk back.

'Find me a priest, we're going to get wed,' he excitedly announced to the entire listening public of Wolverhampton and the Black Country.

What the hell had I just gone and done? Seems like I would do anything to get a reaction on the radio. Hardly a valid reason to get married, yet I couldn't deny that I had become strangely entranced by him. I've heard it's not unusual for stuff like this to happen at work.

I pressurized him not to hang around until the wedding, and we moved in together soon after the proposal. It was only then that I truly understood the meaning of the saying "you never know somebody until you live with them". Whereas he had been perky and attentive and fun to be with while we were in company or on air, no sooner had we shut the door of our cosy little home on the outside world than he became moody and miserable. It was as if, the moment he set foot in our historic terraced house, somebody pressed an off switch in his head. The house was one of a group of six all side by side in downtown Wolverhampton – kind of intimate by American standards, and relevant to our story, in case you're getting bored with my meanderings about English architecture.

So I tried to restore Stan the Man to the man I knew and loved from our lunchtime show. At first I was riddled with guilt, certain his moods were somehow my fault, worrying in the way that women do that there must something wrong with me. Only when people came to visit did he even begin to resemble something like his old self, as if he was only happy when performing to an audience, and the audience of one I represented didn't really count. And please remember, I was going to marry this guy, and a date had already been set, thankfully still around eight months away.

Surely it was no more than the usual getting-to-know-you teething troubles? We were still fabulous on air – after all, we were Stan and Caro from the radio, whose relationship had been nurtured by our listeners.

No, I don't blame you for being curious about our sex life – it's only natural. Just to say that after an enthusiastic first few liaisons he began to lose his spark. Soon he was barely going through the motions before rolling over to close his eyes and nod off. Not so much a sex addict as a sleep addict.

'Wakey wakey, rise and shine,' I would whisper into his ear, to no effect. This was not something I'd ever previously experienced in my life as a southern belle. I could have learnt to live with his impression of Rip Van Winkle if he hadn't begun to mount a campaign of control over me in his waking hours. Maybe he was compensating for his winkle in the bedroom by bigging himself up elsewhere – more Tiny Tim than Big Ben, to quote local parlance – dictating how I should dress, drink, eat and talk to other people, especially men.

I had become caught in a trap, entirely of Stan's making. It was enough to drive a girl to desperation, when in truth all I ever wanted was to live happily ever after with my husband-to-be.

It all came to a head when I received a telephone call from Dot, the landlady of our local pub, the Old Bull and Bush, who had looked on me fondly from the very first time we met, although she had always been more cautious about Stan. It stood at the end of our block, what they call a traditional British boozer, and it was the one place Stan and I regularly visited when we weren't presenting our show.

Dot had always been really welcoming, so when she asked if I would come to her aid behind the bar because one of her barmaids hadn't showed up for the late evening shift, I didn't hesitate. Plus, I thought it would put a smile on Stan's face when he saw me pulling pints. Who knows, I thought, it might even re-ignite our sex life, role-playing customer and barmaid together. Anything to help get our mojo back.

'Crikey, look at you! You really look the part,' said Dot when I reported for duty. I admit to being a little surprised when she suggested that I should use a redder shade of lipstick, rising to shocked on her insistence that I should undo another button on my already tight-fitting cerise blouse. 'If you've got it, flaunt it,' was her justification. I don't believe it came from anywhere deeply sleazy, just something to do with British customs.

'Oh my, Miss Dorothy, but ah'm betrothed to be married to a gentleman!' I said in mock shock, in my best southern drawl. Perhaps I shouldn't have been surprised by the pub regulars who picked up on our conversation, only too keen to join in the debate on Dot's side. Even the wives and girlfriends were voting for me to unbutton. It's their tradition, you see, and who was I to dismiss tradition?

The room went strangely silent for a pub near to closing time, all eyes now focused on me.

'What's a girl to do? It's *sooooo* warm in here. Oh fiddle-dee-dee,' I said. Then I began unbuttoning, to the acclaim of the assembled drinkers.

Except for one. Yes, you guessed it. Stan had walked into the bar at the moment of my mini-striptease. Isn't it always the way?

I didn't blame him for being a little concerned on discovering me entertaining the punters on the wrong side of the bar, but I had at least expected him to get the joke upon hearing my side of the story.

'What do you think you're doing?' he thundered. If looks could kill, I'd have been dead and buried with the wake in full swing. 'You're not only making an exhibition of yourself, it reflects badly on me too.'

'But it's traditional darling. It's like Madonna with Guy Ritchie when she moved to the UK, experiencing the English way of life.'

'Why would you want to compare yourself with that old slag?'

'She's a legend.'

'Leg end more like.'

'I thought we could indulge ourselves in a little fun, with you pretending to be a horny customer and me agreeing to go back to your place for a spot of your British rumpy pumpy,' I said, trying to lighten the tone.

'Well I'd prefer it if you cover up babes. Just look at the way some of those guys are staring at your chest. It's so wrong!'

Womanly confidence can be a fragile thing, and having been diminished by the one I loved, I ran back home to our nearby house to change into the most unappealing, baggy old grey sweater I could find.

'Is that sexless enough for you?' I asked Stan upon my return, and for the benefit of anybody else within earshot.

'Whoa! Don't blame me guys!' he replied addressing the bar, desperate not to lose his popularity with the customers there.

I would love to have put it down to nothing more than good old-fashioned jealousy on his part. I wasn't about to fall out of love with him and consign him to history over something that trivial. And you had to make allowances, because as Tammy Wynette once sang, after all, he was just a man.

But that incident in the pub was only the beginning. It was as if my presence behind the bar had unlocked some primeval urge within him to try and de-sexify me. At first I lamely rolled over and let him have his way as he began to dictate how I dressed at the radio station, the pub, even at home, criticizing the length of my skirts – too short – the color, too loud – and the cut, too tight.

And it didn't stop there. Although we spent pretty much every minute of the day with one another, those extremely rare times when I enjoyed some me time he would interrogate me like I was a girl under suspicion of leading a double life as a hooker in the afternoon, instead of a woman returning from a shopping trip to the local mall.

I'd never felt more imprisoned – except the only crime I'd committed was to be Stan's devoted girlfriend. How dare I be attractive to others?

I even considered escaping in the middle of the night when he was sound asleep, the only time he wasn't monitoring exactly what I was wearing, doing, saying. He was such a heavy sleeper that I sometimes wondered whether he hadn't died.

And then, just when I was at the lowest point of my despair, something quite wonderful happened. This incredible guy moved in next door, and from the first time I saw him, I longed to be in his arms.

Now this wasn't like me. I was going to take my upcoming vows to be faithful deeply seriously, which gives you some indication of how desperate I had become.

I looked out from our spare bedroom over the garden in awestruck admiration, drinking in this mouthwatering man in tight-fitting denims. When he slowly removed his sweatshirt to reveal his impressively muscular, seriously male torso, so honed and buffed and masculine – well, it wasn't a question of when or where or why but exactly how I was going to get to know this guy better.

But what if he wouldn't give me a second glance?

Still, I couldn't stop devouring him with my eyes. And hey, where's the harm in looking?

'What are you doing up there?' I heard Stan shouting from downstairs.

Drooling over a real man, I wanted to reply, *one who doesn't need to keep his wife or girlfriend under 24-hour surveillance to prove he's all male.*

'Just stripping the beds,' I meekly replied instead.

That gave me a further fifteen minutes without interruption. I'd been driven to act this way. Stan's possessiveness was tipping me over the edge, making me lust after another man, but what a man!

I watched the sweat trickle down his broad, manly back as he scythed his way through the overgrown garden, his strong arms sweeping across that jungle of a back yard. I adored the sheer manliness of him. He was so different from Stan, who was still a boy, and not necessarily a very likeable one at that. I wanted to go down and claim this man as my own.

I crouched down so I was hidden by a chair, my eyes just peeping over the top of it so I could continue to enjoy the swish of his scythe and the mesmeric movement of his torso. By now it must be drenched in sweat. My fingers crept to the waistband of my jeans and reached down inside. I imagined licking him dry. I began pleasuring myself even more intensely, until finally I let out a scream as loud as an Eastern European tennis player. I've always been a bit noisy when it comes to sex.

'Are you sure you're OK up there?' I heard Stan enquire.

'Couldn't be better,' I shouted down to him. 'I never knew housework could be so much fun.'

'If you say so,' he replied. Then the phone rang and I heard him take the call. Great, now I could concentrate on making myself climax again. His swagger, his power, his shoulders, his arms, his strength, his butt, his bulge… Oh God! I screamed again, this time so loud that it attracted the attention of the object of my desire. He stopped scything and looked up at me from the garden, and our eyes met. I gave him a little wave of the fingers, mouthing the word 'SPIDER' to explain my unexpected outburst.

'What the hell is going on up there?' shouted Stan, breaking off from his phone call.

'Just a really gross spider,' I called back down to him. 'You know how much I hate the darn things.'

'Do you want me to help you finish it off?' he enquired.

'No need. I've already seen to it myself,' I replied. 'You get back to your phone call.'

So he continued chatting away to somebody at the radio station about him needing to rush in to cover for a DJ who had been taken ill.

Did you know that the clitoris has 8,000 nerve endings compared with only 4,000 for the penis? Well it's true. I tried to compose myself while hastily adjusting my clothing as if nothing of any significance had happened.

'Do you want to come into the studio with me, babes?' Stan enquired of me as I joined him downstairs at the kitchen table. 'They want me to do a one-hander, but you could do traffic and weather if you like.'

'I think I'll pass on that. I've got one of my heads coming on.'

'You do look a little flushed,' he said.

'Oh really?' I replied all innocently.

'But how are you going to keep yourself occupied, babes?' he enquired.

'More housework I guess. I'm really getting to like it. It's better than sex.'

And he thought I was joking.

As soon as he was out the door, I sprinted into the kitchen and poured out a giant pitcher of lemonade, accompanied by a plate of chocolate brownies to be delivered on a tray to our neighbor for his delectation and pleasure. How I like that word pleasure – it was exactly what I wanted to give him, and me.

So I didn't hold back. I put on extra mascara and a slash of red lipstick and changed back into that revealing blouse Stan had earlier shamed me from wearing – that would show him, if had been there to see it. And then at the last moment I decided to step into some ridiculously high heels, so inappropriate for a walk in the back garden on a sunny Sunday afternoon. I'd be swaying provocatively, I hoped, as I walked down the garden carrying refreshments for the gorgeous man.

Not that I was in the habit of propositioning semi-naked guys, at least not without much angst-ridden debate on my part about the rights and wrongs of it. I knew I had exactly 2 hours 40 minutes before Stan was going to walk back in through that door, so I had to act quickly.

'Hey neighbor, you look like a guy who could use a drink and a bite to eat,' I greeted him.

'How kind,' he replied as he looked up, an expression of surprise on his face. It broke into a lazy, sexy smile as he watched me tottering towards him. 'That's really so thoughtful of you,' he added. His deep dark brown voice produced tingles in my tummy and cravings further south. Thank heavens he didn't sound like David Beckham, although he looked as good, if not a shade sexier. He had a rugged, seasoned look about him that told me he was a little older than me and Stan. All the better – I love older men.

'Oh just being a good neighbor,' I said. He started to

put his shirt back on. 'No need to on my account,' I shamelessly added with a grin. Oh no, that was going too far. 'Oh hush my mouth. And me an engaged woman,' I said. I was starting to babble.

'Well, if it doesn't offend you,' he said, taking it back off again. I took the opportunity of carrying out my very own three-point examination while he disrobed. Wedding band? I'm afraid so. Big hands – excellent. And a tight, muscular derriere – yes sirree! Well, two out of three ain't bad.

'Please allow me to introduce myself. I'm Larry,' he said, offering me his hand.

'I'm Caroline, but my friends call me Caro,' I replied.

He squeezed my hand tightly. 'Pleased to meet you, Caro,' he said, squeezing me once again. I was fantasizing about where he might want to squeeze me next.

'You know, I'm sure I've heard your voice before,' he went on. 'Not just because you're a Yank.'

'I'm from the South actually, raised in Atlanta, Georgia', I said, instantly regretting coming over as a pedant. '*Gone with the Wind* and all that – just think of me as Scarlett O'Hara without the racism'.

'That's it, I've got it. You sound exactly like that gorgeous lady on the radio. You know, the one who's on with that complete idiot on Radio Wolfie at lunchtime.'

'Oh, you mean my fiancé,' I said chuckling.

'Oh dear,' he said smiling. 'I didn't mean any offence. Fancy me living next door to a celebrity.'

'And I'm sure he would like to meet you,' I replied.

'No, not him. You're the famous one.'

'Well I'm sure he'd like to meet you anyway,' I replied. I could feel myself coloring up.

'Why not? I'd be delighted.'

'So – what about this evening, then?'

'Great! I'll bring a bottle of wine.'

'That would be great. And your wife too,' I added, casting a look in the direction of his ring finger.

'She won't be coming, I'm afraid. We're taking a break from one other. That's why I'm moving in here alone, while she and the kids stay at home in Lichfield. So it will just be me on my own, I'm afraid.'

I struggled to hide my elation. I would have him all to myself, give or take Stan.

'Eight o' clock then, don't be late,' I said with a girlish giggle. My gaze kept returning to his scrumptious torso. If only my feelings were reciprocated. I saw him take a glance at my low-cut sweater and sensed there could be hope. And then a swirl of erotically-charged thoughts flooded my mind, releasing a rush of red hot blood to my extremities. I realised in sheer horror that my nipples had become more visibly pronounced than was appropriate for a genteel Sunday afternoon stroll in the garden with your neighbor.

'Must dash,' I said. How utterly embarrassing.

'Would you like your tray back?' he asked.

'How thoughtful,' I said, and accepted it from his strong hands before using it as a shield to cover my chest. I sashayed back towards the house to prepare our home – and myself – for his visit, leaving him to his gardening.

What must he have thought of me? So forward – desperate, even. I felt ashamed of myself. But then, what man isn't warmed by the sight of a woman's arousal, surely the most natural thing in the world? And besides, those blessed nipples were beyond my control. Please let him approve of me, I prayed. I yearned to be ravished by him. Look, I know what you're thinking, but really it was no more than a stupid fantasy. I was well on the road to marrying sweet, likeable Stan, and nothing was going to deflect me from my commitment. Sure, I'd had a few issues with Stan's control freakery, but it wasn't anything I couldn't resolve, and shagging the next-door neighbor is such a cliché anyway. I was far too sophisticated for all that. Wasn't I?

Stan was not especially pleased when I told him that I had invited the new neighbor around for drinks. 'Oh God, I'm shattered,' he said. He was always tired, except when he was sleeping. 'You don't fancy him, do you?' he added with a hint of alarm in his voice. 'That wouldn't be your reason for inviting him?'

'Now you're being ridiculous. He's old enough to be my – er – older brother. I only invited him because he's on his own. I felt sorry for him – that's all. And it's the neighborly thing to do, isn't it?'

'In the US maybe, but not here in England. We Brits like to keep ourselves to ourselves.'

'And he just loves your radio show. He told me how much he enjoys listening to it.'

Stan's expression warmed a little at that. 'Oh well, in

that case, I suppose it would be rude not to,' he said. He was never able to resist the lure of an audience, even if it was only one person.

Larry turned up later as arranged, with an expensive bottle of Burgundy in one hand and a big bunch of flowers for me in the other. Stan was more impressed by the wine than the flowers. I guess for me it was the other way around.

After Stan had finished giving Larry an extensive resume of his career and how he'd built up the best audience on local commercial radio in the UK, I eventually got to ask our neighbor the questions I had been longing to pose all evening.

'So, what brings you here to sunny Wolverhampton on your own?' I said.

'It's complicated. My wife and I are having this trial separation after fifteen years of marriage, to see if we can't work things out. I think she's had enough of me.'

'I find that hard to believe,' I said with just a touch too much force, although Stan only managed to stifle a yawn.

'She gets infuriated by what she describes as my lack of a career plan. I prefer to write about tranquil countryside pursuits, and I also edit *British Waterways Magazine*. She would prefer me to go back to my old career in show business journalism. You can make loads of money writing stupid stories about pointless celebrities doing dumb things, but it doesn't float my boat. You see, I'm a country boy at heart.'

'Ahhhhhh,' I sighed.

'Country boy, that's pushing it! You must be at least 40!' Stan rudely observed.

Larry just smiled kindly. 'I'm 38, actually. I suppose that must seem ancient to you young people.'

'You're still in the prime of life, Larry,' I assured him. 'I'm sure that if your wife is crazy enough not to want you, then pretty girls will be lining up to carry on where she left off.'

Had I gone too far with my vote of confidence? I didn't think Stan looked too bothered. He probably assumed that Larry was much too old to be floating the boat of a hip twenty-two-year-old American chick like me. Big mistake. The control freak had taken his eye off the ball – or should I say balls.

'You've been so welcoming to me,' said Larry as he prepared to leave, 'that if I should ever run out of sugar I know exactly who to call.'

'Mighty pleased to be of service,' I replied in my finest southern accent. I was desperate to see him again.

After that first glorious meeting there followed a number of fleeting moments when our paths crossed, but Stan was never too far away.

'Hi, how are you settling in?' I would shout out after him.

What I wanted him to say was 'Loving it, I've dumped the wife, and I'm ready for some action'. Instead it would be, 'Oh, bearing up. So kind of you to ask.'

I feared he still loved her. I began to think I was losing my mind. I even considered risking my relationship with my much admired and hugely popular fiancé. Slowly I began the task of erasing Larry from my thoughts as a potential lover, reappraising and recategorizing him as just a neighbor and a married man who would soon be returning to live with his lovely devoted wife.

Then one day, when I had just about calmed down and got myself back on track on the road to Marriageville, I was sitting sedately next to Stan in the Old Bull and Bush bar when along came Larry, looking fit and fuckable as ever in his tightly-packed jeans and short sleeve checked shirt, unbuttoned enough to show off his rippling chest, ordering a pint of cider at the bar.

'Oh no, it's the guy from next door again,' said Stan. 'Let's keep our heads down before he comes over to join us. Who wants to be stuck with a loser like that? Too late,' he said under his breath as Larry politely asked if he could join us.

'It would be a pleasure, wouldn't it, Stan?'

'Yes, sure thing, babes,' Stan reluctantly concurred. He used the moment as an excuse to take a bathroom break before being stopped on his way by one of the pub regulars who wanted to ask him a question about the quiz on yesterday's show. And Stan could never ever resist talking to a fan.

Larry and I must have had nearly five minutes of precious time alone together. He asked me how my day had been, and listened intently to me blathering on about not being able to find the right kind of bulb for a particular light fitting. How fascinating I must have seemed.

Then he waxed lyrically about his recent trip photographing the glories of the Grand Union Canal, holding me spellbound as he spoke so adorably about his journey along this great British waterway. I so wanted to go there with him. Then he mentioned his most recent visit to his estranged wife.

'How did it go?' I ventured to ask him.

'Frosty,' he replied.

I struggled not to high-five him in celebration. You could say I wasn't exactly what you would call a well-wisher when it came to repairing his marriage. 'Poor you,' I said instead, but not nearly enough like I meant it.

I went over to the bar to buy a round of drinks, and Dot leaned over and said something that changed the course of history: 'You two look really good together.'

'I should hope so. We're getting married in six months' time,' I dismissively replied.

'No, not Stan, silly. I mean you and your neighbor. You look like you really belong to one another.'

I was nonplussed, yet if she could see it – and Dot was an exceptionally wise woman of the type I would one day like to become – then maybe I hadn't become delusional after all. And in case I needed any more persuading she added: 'Sometimes a girl in her prime has to look elsewhere when she can't find love at home.'

'Why Miss Dot, I do declare I'm about as shook up as a southern belle has a right to be by the outrageous implications of your words.'

'He'd be so good for you.'

How could I possibly disagree with her?

'But what if he shouldn't fall for my womanly charms?'

'That's the least of your worries. You're gorgeous dear, in case you'd forgotten.'

How sweet of her, but embarrassing too. I paused for a short while as I considered my next question.

'So, how can you be so sure that Larry wants me?'

'An older woman's intuition. Or could it be that that twinkle in his eye whenever he sees you?'

'Are you serious?'

'You really haven't noticed the effect you're having upon him? It's like, get a room, as I've heard you Americans say.'

'Dot! You're a disgrace.' We both dissolved into laughter, giggling like a couple of adolescent girls.

So, just when I thought I'd successfully lowered the temperature of my feelings towards my red-hot neighbor, Dot just stokes up the goddam fire. If an onlooker like her could sense our sexual chemistry, how could I continue to deny the spark between Larry and me?

'What's so funny?' Stan asked upon my return, still monitoring my every move.

'Girly stuff. Nothing that would interest you, babes.'

'Too much information already,' he replied, showing me the hand.

As I lay in bed that night, Larry only a wall's width away, I imagined what it would it would be like to sashay into his bedroom dressed in my sexiest undies, prior to being ravished by him. If only. He might as well have been a thousand miles away. So near, yet so frustratingly far.

When I switched the light off, Stan was already fast

asleep in our bed. He was to sleeping what Stephen Hawking was to black holes – an expert. It would have been easier to have raised the dead once Stan had shut his eyes. He would be impossible to wake for the next seven to eight hours.

I dozed off into a light sleep. It was probably only a matter of minutes before I was woken up by a substantial bang downstairs. Burglars? I jabbed Stan in the ribs to get his attention, without response. He could have slept through an earthquake followed by a volcano. If only Larry had been there to protect me, with his strong manly hands and arms to repel the intruder, and then hold me tight once he'd tied the thief up in knots.

So what would Stan have done? Played the villain a request on his radio show the next day?

There was only one thing for it. I crept out of bed and ventured hesitantly downstairs, an ornamental candlestick in my hand, ready to bludgeon the criminal and give him a splitting headache, if he was lucky. I would have to be careful – maybe it was Larry who had come to claim me. It seemed unlikely, unless he'd managed to enter through the cat flap.

Surely that must have woken Stan up? Yet when I returned to the bedroom he was still dead to the world. I could never feel safe and secure with this guy. He was truly unwakeable.

And then I had a wicked thought. Just suppose I did venture next door in the dark for a midnight assignation with Larry. Would Stan even know?

I seriously thought about going for it there and then, all fired up as I was by the fear and excitement of thinking we'd had an intruder. But then I thought better of it. A couple more trial runs were required before I dared do such a thing. Besides, although it might seem deeply shallow, I also wanted to look my best. A visit to a top lingerie emporium seemed the least I could do.

Twenty-four hours later, with military precision and meticulous planning, I began my campaign to secure the ultimate night of passion with my neighbour. I waited until Stan was safe in the land of nod, then I pinched his butt; nothing. Then his forearm, followed by his leg. Still nothing – so far so good. Next I tweaked his nose. There was just a swift shake of the head and an interruption to the steady flow of snores before he quickly resumed the rhythm of his sleep.

Next I began whispering inappropriate stuff about Larry, praising all his manly virtues, as if I was trying to speak to him through the wall where he lay only a few yards away. Stan paid as much attention as a stuffed dinosaur.

And so the night of decision arrived. It was the perfect storm – the right time of the month, some breathtaking new Victoria's Secret lingerie, my hair newly cut and styled, my mind set on only one thing.

Of course doubts began to plague me, such as – did Larry really feel about me the way I thought of him? What if he still loved his wife, and told me to get the hell out of his room and stop acting like a whore and go back to my husband in waiting? How could I ever face myself in the mirror again if he did?

As bad luck would have it, Stan exhibited the faintest of signs of becoming amorous on the night in question.

'I've got a splitting headache, babes,' I begged of him.

I didn't usually have to bother with excuses, such was his lack of interest in me. He almost looked relieved upon hearing it, happily turning over for his preferred passion, a good night's sleep.

Job done, although I gave it another ten minutes until the snoring began. I lay back and imagined Larry having me.

Soon I decided it was safe for me to creep out of our bed. I made my way straight to the spare room, where I rid myself of my PJs and slipped into a shamelessly provocative animal print lace garter slip. I didn't want to leave Larry in any doubt as to the nature of my call.

Next, I applied a healthy slash of scarlet lipstick, some high-precision liquid eyeliner, plentiful mascara and some smoky eye shadow. I wanted to appear provocative without looking cheap. Then finally I removed my engagement ring, so symbolic of the place I was in.

There could be no turning back. By now I wanted him so badly it hurt. I was longing for him to be inside me more than I'd ever craved a man before – it must be lust. I had an itch that needed scratching so bad, and only Larry could see to it.

I looked up to see a subdued light shining out of his bedroom window. Guided by it, I tiptoed cautiously across our backyard into his. In my right hand I was carrying a bowl. If I was going to run back home, now was my last chance to do it, but the magnetic pull of the promise of Larry was far greater than any fear my conscience or common sense could drum up to deter me.

I stood outside his house wondering whether I had taken leave of my senses, but I knew I had to see this thing through.

I knocked on his door, lightly at first. No reply. I banged a little harder, and this time I heard his footsteps come tip-tapping along the stone floor, heading in my direction. Oh god! What in heaven's name was I doing there? I was an engaged woman with a fiancé sleeping only a short distance away from me. Had I no shame? Obviously not. Sometimes a girl has to follow her heart.

The door opened in front of me.

'Sugar?' I sweetly enquired, holding the bowl out towards him for his delectation.

He smiled knowingly. He was looking totally adorable in his figure-hugging T-shirt and tight-fitting shorts. I knew I'd made the right decision. Our attraction was mutual and immediate, and if he hadn't stepped forward to hold me in his strong muscular arms and kiss me passionately on my mouth, I would have thrown myself at him instead. I preferred it that way round though, with him taking the initiative. After all, I'd made all the first moves so far, and now I wanted to be fucked by him as my reward.

He held me so tightly I could barely breathe. I could feel the outline of what felt like a hugely impressive cock pressing urgently against me. 'Back of the net,' as they say around these parts when Wolverhampton Wanderers score a goal.

'I wanted you from the moment I first saw you in the garden wielding your scythe,' I said as he led me upstairs to his bedroom, separated by just a few feet of air and some bricks from where Stan lay sleeping on the other side of the wall.

'Then what kept you?' he replied with a wink. He asked me to wait a short while, and then he reappeared. He lifted me off my feet with his strong manly arms and carried me into his bedroom. I was totally taken aback by the sight of his double bed. It was surrounded by scented candles, and covered in rose petals. Was he a romantic or a serial killer? How the hell did he know I was coming?

'What's this?' I asked.

'Every night since I first realised there was something between us I hoped and prayed you might visit me like this. So I began to prepare. I never meant to be presumptuous. I only wanted it to be special.'

Phew – he was a romantic.

'It's so beautiful. It's as if you can read my mind,' I reassured him. 'And you can read my body too.' He slipped my nightdress above my head and held me tightly in another passionate embrace, his tongue playfully entering and exiting my mouth. How I loved the taste of him – it was man, pure and simple, yet divinely so. And how I needed his utter manliness to remind me I was all woman. I wanted to be pleasured and teased, enticed and then fucked by a real man, not some wining boy.

He unclipped my bra with the dexterity of a guy who knew how to use his fingers, heralding the promise of heightened pleasure ahead. And as he sucked my nipples, I unleashed the first of my many moans, each one getting louder than the last. I wondered if I would wake Stan up, and he would find himself alone in our bed listening to me climaxing next door. But I didn't care. I loved the danger of it as Larry's finger slipped so cleverly and confidently inside me, knowing exactly where I loved to be touched, like he'd read a manual on me, sensing exactly which buttons to press. So unlike Stan, who was more like a tourist on holiday in a foreign city, lost without a map.

Then the tip of his tongue caressed my clit, causing bursts of pleasure to pulse through those eight thousand nerve endings. Omigod, I'd never experienced anything quite that intense, nor had I screamed that loud either. It was so piercing it shook the window pane.

'Shush!' he gently urged me.

'Don't worry, he'll be sound asleep,' I said. That must have made him wonder whether I'd either drugged or perhaps murdered him. Well, you do read about these things.

Larry proceeded to explore every inch of my body, licking and kissing then licking me again until I was alive with sex. When he began to reach for his Calvin Kleins, I was unable to wait any longer, and ripped them off for him.

'Now that is what a real man is supposed to look like,' I said loudly.

'Shush!' he urged me once again.

'I'm dying of pleasure here!' I yelled as he entered me. He inhabited me so completely that I wanted to own his awesome cock, to keep it inside me forever.

How I adored the intense highs and laid-back lows of the ever-changing rhythms of his varied thrusts, as if he knew the exact force and the precise motion I needed at any particular time. It was almost mystic. You've heard of a mind reader; well, this man was a vagina reader, I reflected, as I came for what seemed like the 25th time. And I was his cock whisperer, enticing it to explode and then to luxuriate in those cascades of liquid love flowing deep inside of me, while his big manly roar reverberated thrillingly in my ears. And I didn't tell him to shush, either.

He'd completed me. I lay in his arms, feeling like a natural-born woman is supposed to feel, while he ran his hand lightly through my hair and kissed me softly on the neck.

'So where do we go from here?' he asked, when it was all over and we lay nestled together.

I didn't really know. So when in doubt, stroke your lover's humungous balls.

I guess I've objectified my neighbor enough times for your delight by now. You want some more? I know I certainly did. So I'll simply say we made love again, a little less frenetically but no less passionately second time around. We enjoyed one another until morning began to break.

'I better get back before Stan wakes up,' I said apologetically. Hardly the most romantic thing I'd ever said.

'I do hope you will come and visit again,' he said with that touch of old school English hospitality of his which I found so endearing.

'It would be rude not to,' I graciously concurred.

'I feel so much sweeter for it,' he said, handing me back an empty sugar bowl.

'I will be counting the hours,' I replied before giving him a lingering kiss on the lips. It felt ridiculously counter-intuitive to tear myself away from him. Finally I forced myself to disentangle myself from his embrace and make my way home, stopping at our spare room to change into my sensible pajamas and remove all traces of make-up. I was now ready to slip back into bed with Stan, who was still mercifully fast asleep.

Within what seemed like seconds the alarm clock sounded, and Stan stirred. He yawned loudly as he struggled to regain consciousness, and then stretched his arms in the air.

'Did you sleep well, babes?' he asked me.

'Never better – I had the most wonderful dream, so vivid it could have been real.'

'You can't beat a good night, can you babes? It sets you up for the day ahead.'

'I can't get enough of it,' I gladly confessed. Wrong on so many levels, I know.

While I should have felt shame, my overriding emotion was elation at having got away with it. The prospect of countless more nights to come in the arms of Larry outweighed any guilt I might feel.

After that, Larry and I continued to meet up almost every night, and if anything the sex got better. In between, we even found time to talk. He spoke so tenderly of his concerns about the effect the trial separation might be having upon his two children. And he was happy to listen to me blathering on about my dilemma with Stan, never feeling the need to come up with definitive answers, apart from saying that everybody deserved happiness in their lives, and that nobody should ever be afraid to pursue their dream.

'I can't imagine what I've done to deserve you,' he was always telling me, while I would forever thank him for rescuing me from my despair. I just loved being with him. I longed to reveal our love in a world where I could openly walk alongside him, proudly proclaiming my ownership of that awesome manly persona, that rugged face, those broad shoulders, the strong back, the cute little bottom, and everything else I cherished about him.

Perhaps it would have remained our guilty secret forever had not Dot intervened, just as real remorse was beginning to kick in again. Maybe it was something to do with my strict religious upbringing, or the shame of what I was doing behind Stan's back, or perhaps I just couldn't cope with this much sheer bliss in my life. Whatever the reason, I had decided I was going to have to give Larry up, assuming he didn't dump me first.

But Dot had other ideas.

'I've never seen you look happier, my dear,' she said on one of the few occasions Stan permitted me go to the bar to buy drinks on my own. 'On no account must you let him slip away.'

How could I possibly let Larry go after receiving the unambiguous backing of such a wise and worldly woman as Dot? I believe she recognized that I had found a man who embodied all those great old-fashioned masculine values of showing respect towards women, being emotionally strong while able to fix stuff around the house, eschewing vanity yet keeping his body in great shape, being a selfless lover, having taken the time to know exactly how women work, being modest and making me feel protected while giving me the space to be me. What's not to like?

Of course I still continued to suffer from occasional bouts of guilt, thinking about how I was deceiving Stan, making love with another man while he lay there sleeping. Not exactly how I'd expected to be treating my fiancé when I was an idealistic teenager, but hadn't Stan brought most of this on himself with his controlling behavior? The more he tried to control me, the more I wanted to disobey him. And the more controlling Stan became, the more attractive Larry appeared. Trouble was, I now wanted Larry night and day, but Stan was an inescapable presence during waking hours, always by my side.

But then I had another slice of good fortune – our radio station unexpectedly announcing the launch of a series of summer road shows around the region, and I wasn't required.

'You go for it, Stan,' I said. 'You know how much I hate live appearances, and you're so brilliant at them.'

'I can't deny that I've got a gift for the live show,' said Stan, whereas you...'

'You don't have to say it.'

'But how will you pass the time while I'm away?'

Fucking a gorgeous man.

No, I didn't actually say that.

'I could help Dot in the pub,' I suggested.

The way he reacted, I might as well have said 'fucking a gorgeous man'.

'No way. I refuse to have all those creeps gawping at you.'

So then I took fate in my hand.

'Well perhaps Larry could accompany me to the Bush for a drink and a meal. He'd be the perfect chaperone while you're away.'

'What a great idea, babes. And maybe he could take you for a ride on that boat of his. He's always going on about it. What a bore. I hear he has an incredibly long but narrow one.'

'No it's wide as well as long, that's the best thing about it,' I said. I wanted to add, *and he can keep it going for hours*. I had to turn away so he wouldn't notice my grin.

Just because Larry was knocking on forty, he might as well have been entrusting me to the care of his grandfather, such was Stan's take on him.

So magically, Larry and I had the opportunity to sit opposite one another in the Old Bull and Bush, staring into one another's eyes over a pint of cider and a jacket potato, touching each other far more frequently than friends ever would, while Dot smiled at us warmly from behind the bar.

Soon the locals who drank there began to work out there must be something going on between us. Rather than being shocked or judgmental, they enthusiastically endorsed our affair and gladly accepted us as an item. And that felt good to me, making us believe that it was meant to be, not some sordid little secret to be kept hidden from the rest of the world.

When the pub regulars lined up to wave us off outside the Bush as we drove away to set sail on Larry's boat, it felt like we were a couple of newly-weds leaving for our honeymoon. I'd never felt this happy, or that insatiable too, and the more he gave, the more I wanted.

As we wended our way through the delightfully gentle English countryside, unable to keep our hands off one another when we should have been concentrating on navigating the locks, it became our very own Love Boat.

It seemed our luck had finally run out when Stan insisted that he should join us on one of our cruises – not because he suspected anything was going on between us, but in fear that he might be missing out on a free trip. Suddenly we had to create the impression we'd been sleeping in separate cabins, with me and my fiancé now frustratingly consigned to guest quarters. But that was only until Stan obligingly fell into a coma at bedtime, when I was once again able to rejoin my hunk in his bunk.

I could barely look Stan in the eye the next morning when he started going on about some strange rocking movements he'd felt in the middle of the night.

'It must have been an enormous fish swimming by,' I said.

'In a canal?'

'More likely a tidal wave,' Larry suggested, only slightly more convincingly.

It was moments like these that made me seriously wonder how long we could keep it up before we were found out. For most of the time Larry and I lived in our own little bubble, but it couldn't last. As my wedding day grew ever closer, reality threatened to destroy our weird ménage-à-trois.

Meanwhile, having momentously decided that he was never going back to his wife, Larry set about initiating divorce proceedings, and was now free to hook up with me, assuming I had the courage to dump Stan. It was a no-brainer, yet still I couldn't do it. And much as I loved and lusted after Larry, I couldn't seem to free myself from Stan's all-encompassing influence.

It was as if I had committed a dreadful sin by sleeping with Larry and now I had to atone for it by marrying Stan. It was my penance.

'I'm so, so, sorry, but I'm going to have to end it,' I told Larry on our last ever night-time assignation together.

'I've made a commitment to Stan and I refuse to let him down,' I added, in defiance of my feelings.

He begged me to see sense, but nothing anybody could say would make me change my mind, not even Dot.

'You two were made for each other and you've got your whole life ahead of you,' she pleaded with me. 'And he's got great balls.'

'Dot!' I exclaimed in shock horror. Now when did I ever tell her that?

However, I refused to give up on my fiancé, and they knew it, which might explain why one evening Stan walked into our kitchen to announce that Larry had accepted his invitation to become Best Man.

'Oh great. I didn't think you were that keen on him,' I said, trying to disguise how angry I was that Larry had agreed to this request. I was suspecting some sort of revenge on his part. Maybe that's what fired me up to ask Dot to give me away, and astonishingly, she agreed, without any warnings, such as was I doing the right thing in marrying Stan, or anything like that. She said she'd be only too happy.

When the big day arrived Larry looked so super handsome that I could barely take my eyes off him, whereas I hardly noticed Stan as I walked up the aisle in the wedding suite of the George Hotel. Yes, people may have mentioned that I looked the part, although that's barely relevant the way things turned out. So what the hell was I doing, getting married to Stan? It was far, far crazier than slipping next door to fuck my neighbor while my fiancé slept alone in our marital bed. But I was determined to go through with this wedding, however insane it might seem, to wash myself clean of the guilt of forsaking Stan for Larry's arms.

When the Registrar began to read all the official oaths, asking my fiancé to pledge his love for me, a strange thing happened. Stan stayed resolutely silent. What was he playing at?

The Registrar leaned forward and mouthed the words 'I will' at Stan, but still he refused to say them. Instead he drew a deep breath and solemnly declared, 'I'm so sorry everybody, but it's more a case of 'I won't'.'

'Stan! How could you?' I stared at him, my eyes like daggers on stalks.

'Sorry babes,' he said. 'I know how crazy you are for me, and just how much it will break your heart, but I'm really not sure I can deal with this whole commitment thing. It took a very wise woman to make me understand that I'm not ready to be a husband to you, or anybody else.' Then he looked up... at Dot.

So that was it. Dot had talked him out of it. A small part of me could have killed her, but only a small part.

I took Stan's hand, looking at him more warmly than any time since the day he'd first proposed to me on air. In fact, get in, as they also said round there when Wolverhampton Wanderers scored another goal. Well, it was hardly the time to bring up such issues as my unusual sleeping arrangements, was it? It would have been unkind, and in my book, kindness was a greater virtue than needless honesty, if not the greatest virtue of them all.

'Maybe you're right Stan,' I said. 'Some things just aren't meant to be. I do appreciate you speaking your mind, sweetheart, although it would have been nice if you could have given me a little prior warning.'

'You're so right babes,' he replied. 'I'll tell you what – I'll play a few tunes for you at the reception as my way of saying sorry. No charge. It's on me.'

'Reception? How on earth can we have a reception when you've just jilted me?

'Well, it's a shame to see it go to waste.'

'If you say so,' I lamely replied.

'Frankly my dear, I don't give a damn about the reception,' said Larry, intervening out of the blue, looking so mighty fine in his black Pierre Cardin suit.

'So, if you're not ready for her Stan,' he said. He was walking purposefully and manfully towards me. Then he got down on one knee. 'Caroline Shania-Mae Kennedy, will you do me the honour of becoming my wife?'

First, I addressed my fiancé.

'Sorry, Stan, but never has that title of Best Man been more deserved than by Larry.'

I pretended to stall for a moment, holding out my straight index finger underneath my chin and tilting my head to one side while looking upwards to some unidentifiable object on high – the customary pose of a southern belle who has just been asked for her hand in marriage.

'Oh fiddle-dee-dee kind sir, I surely will,' I said. The one hundred guests, who had been on something of an emotional roller coaster up to this point, cheered wildly, mostly in relief.

Stan appeared a little perplexed that I should accept a proposal within seconds of being jilted by him, from a man who he'd always assumed had failed to float my boat. I looked at Dot and mouthed 'thank you' at her. I couldn't help but notice a tear well up in her eye.

Without further ado we all trooped off to the hotel's Great Hall, where Stan played his selection of hits of the eighties for the enjoyment of our still slightly bemused guests while Larry and I took the floor for the first dance. Everybody was cheering and clapping, now that we no longer had to hide our love away.

We danced to one song after another. Much later in the evening we tried to leave unnoticed, and failed miserably. The crowd chanted 'We Know Where You're Going' as Larry whisked me off to make mad passionate love, this time in the hotel's bridal suite. Not that we were married yet, but as my heroine Scarlett O'Hara once famously said, tomorrow is another day.

THE FLIRT

Flirting is better than sex – there, I've said it. Exactly why I was so smitten by entrancing men with honey-coated words, and being entranced by them, I'll tell you later. Just to say that I totally adored flirting. In truth, I was a flirting addict – 'my name is Annie O'Brien and I'm a flirtaholic'. There, it's out, which is all very well, except that you should pity all those poor boyfriends of mine, not to mention those guys I'd been flirting with, because all of them in their different ways expected so much more from me. If only they could have appreciated that it was just a bit of harmless fun, a spine-tingling, thrill-seeking sexual game, but a game nevertheless.

So what was it with guys in their twenties, like me, misconstruing what I'd been playing at? Every one of my ex-boyfriends had been convinced that my flirting was an overture to a full-on sexual symphony with another man, while the object of my flirtatiousness would take everything at face value, believing they had won the Golden Ticket to my pleasure factory. Come on guys – just the thought of it was supposed to be enough!

So no sooner had my boyfriend Gary left me alone in an uptown, upmarket hotel bar while he moved his car than the middle-aged yet seriously handsome businessman turned towards me and flashed me a knowing smile. Perfect – it was time for some sport. I half-smiled back, just enough to urge him on to the next level.

'Is it hot in here, or is it just you?' he quipped.

I grimaced, but affectionately so, like an aunt on hearing her favourite seven-year-old nephew's latest attempt at a joke. I knew he could do better, for when it comes to flirting older guys are in a league of their own. You can forgive a little paunch here, a touch of jowl there and grey hairs everywhere, because it's such a delight to play with an accomplished exponent of the sport of flirting. It's like being paired with Roger Federer after years of playing tennis with park players.

'That young guy – he must be out of his mind, leaving you alone in a place like this,' my new sparring partner went on. Inappropriate, but promising.

'So you don't think I can be trusted on my own?' I smouldered, tilting my head to one side, then flicking my hair. I started him momentarily right between the eyes before averting my gaze.

'Have you heard the expression "while the cat's away, the mice will play?" How are you fixed?'

'That's for me to know and you to find out,' I said, tweaking his metaphorical whiskers.

'Anyway, it's not you he should be worrying about, it's leaving you with guys like me,' he vaingloriously replied.

'You really don't look that dangerous to me,' I observed, putting his claim of being a threat to my virtue to the sword of female mockery.

In the game of flirting, forget all about gender equality. It's the girl who holds all the aces. After all, we've got something he desperately wants, while we wouldn't dream of even thinking of letting him have his way until he has danced beautifully to our tune. And even if he does perform all the right steps, a true flirt – or some would say, a cockteaser – will always teasingly decline, leaving them wanting more.

'Having helped to destroy my self-esteem, would you like to help me to rebuild it?' he asked.

'Ah sweetheart, of course I would – how shall I start? You're adorable,' I said. I moved my bar stool next to his, removing a piece of fluff from the lapel of his jacket. 'If you like that sort of thing,' I added.

Even if he didn't, I certainly did. When it came to flirting you couldn't do better than a stylishly rich older man. They always used to tickle my fancy when it came to playing verbal tennis. But I wasn't about to let him know it, as that would ruin the game. You have to keep them guessing, right until the sweet end.

'Let me buy you a drink,' he said.

'Do you want to get me woozy?' I whispered into his ear.

'And why would I want to do that?'

'To get me to do things I wouldn't do sober.'

'Such as?'

I giggled. 'No, I couldn't possibly,' I stuttered.

'Go on. Spit it out. It's time for whatever you want.'

'Here goes then.' I coughed nervously. 'I would like to stroke your... er... moustache.'

'Well don't let me stop you there,' he said.

'But I'm really an extremely shy kind of girl,' I replied, even summoning up a blush on demand as if to prove the point.

'Bartender!' he commanded. 'A Bollinger for the lady!' The glass came immediately, and he placed it eagerly into my hand.

'Santé,' I toasted him.

'Bottoms up,' he replied. 'And did you know that champagne gets into the central nervous system faster than any other drink, thanks to all those naughty little bubbles?'

'You are so knowledgeable,' I said as I took a sip of the sparkling wine. 'I'm sure there is so much more you could teach me.' I stroked his stylishly-groomed upper lip, just as I'd promised.

'It's my weakness. I just love playing with them,' I confided.

'Is there anything else you would like to play with?'

Now there is always a point where flirting can tip over into something more full on, especially when the flirtee sacrifices innuendo in favor of porn – it's just so uncool when that happens.

'You know there is, you naughty boy,' I said allowing my eyes to drift down to his pants for the shortest of times. 'Your hands. There's nothing more relaxing than a good hand massage. Have no fear, I'm qualified, you know. It's my speciality.'

He appeared confused, which was as it should be. In the game of flirting, the woman should always be half virgin, half whore, constantly putting the guy on the back foot for the duration of the game, unnerving, then exciting, then unsettling him by however much you veer between those two respective poles, going as close to full on whore as your nerve will allow before surging back to shocked-again virgin as his hopes grow higher than his erection.

So I linked my right hand with his, threading my fingers through his, wiggling them backwards and forward. And then at that precise moment, Gary returned from the business with his car.

'I might have guessed,' he began moaning. 'I can't leave you alone for five minutes without you throwing yourself at some slimy old greaseball. You're behaving like a slut.'

'Hey bud, that's no way to speak to a lady,' the middle-aged guy replied.

Ah bless him, not only was he a great flirt, he was chivalrous too.

'Butt out, Grandad. This is none of your frigging business,' said Gary. He was being so un-Dorothy Parker.

'Grow up Gary!' I snapped. 'Haven't you heard of being friendly? And if you will go out with a qualified physical therapist. I was simply giving this charming gentleman a hand massage to help relieve his stress.'

'A hand job, more like.' Gary huffed and puffed. 'I've had it up to hear with you.' On and on and on he went, all the way back home to my apartment. Our romantic dinner for two was now abandoned, at the end of what should have been a really special evening celebrating our first anniversary. And I'm only talking first week here!

It hadn't taken long for Gary to give up on me, because like so many others before him, he just couldn't handle my flirting. OK, so he might have been a touch immature not to see how harmless it really was, but just like all the others he took it as a personal insult against his masculinity, and as we all know, there can be no coming back from that.

Of course, I should have restricted my flirting to the times when I was out on the town with the girls, and be happy to concentrate all my attention on the boy of the moment instead. Quite simply, I was incorrigible – see man, must flirt, but never ever see man, must have sex, as all my previous boyfriends seemed to think.

You might be wondering how I came to be like this. The best way I can describe it is that's it's a defense mechanism, or at least that's how it all started when I first began to frequent bars with my teenage girlfriends. I'm embarrassed to admit it, but whether it was about the way I dressed – quite modestly, I thought – or something to do with the way nature had made me, guys always seemed to pick me out as the one they wanted to tease, torment, and then flatter.

'You're a bundle of fun,' they would often say, a reference to my petite stature, just five feet two inches tall, with my tiny waist, curvaceous bottom and incongruous DD boobs, which really belonged on a much larger framed woman. At first it drove me to despair, as I was unsettled by the effect it was having on friendships with my girlfriends to such an extent that I started to decline invitations to go out. That was until I decided to fight back and give these guys as good as I got, which is pretty much all flirting is. Otherwise how was I ever going to have any kind of social life?

I soon discovered I was good at it, even capable of taking on a whole group of guys, which happened around the time I was going out with Justin, the guy who followed poor Gary.

I guess it's not every day you encounter a bunch of barber shop quartets drinking in a bar when you are on your first date with a new boyfriend. They'd all been participating in the local regional finals – I didn't even know there were such things – and were now celebrating their successes with a bucketload of drinks and a few rousing renditions of timeless classics such as *Nothing Could Be Finer Than To Be In Carolina In The Morning*.

I should have kept my head down and concentrated

on Justin. Sure, the barber shop guys were kind of geeky, but what's not to like about a group of guys with that clean-cut Mormon look? Like, you want to dirty them up a little, and then suddenly, they're performing a song in your honor. How cool is that?

I hadn't asked them to sing about me, but in the time it took Justin to visit the men's room I struck up small talk with some of them. How could I possibly resist? They were the ultimate challenge to a flirt like me.

'What's with the bow ties?' I asked of any guy who would answer. I'd always had a thing about dicky bows.

'We're singers,' replied the guy I'd marked out as being particularly agreeable. 'We've all been competing against each other, but we're all friends now.'

'Well I so approve of that – make love not war, that's my philosophy, and I hope it's yours too.'

'Wow, I guess so,' said the guy, who I soon came to know as Brian, the lead tenor. He was coloring up ever deeper as he spoke.

'And will you be serenading your girlfriend when you get back home?' I asked him.

'I would if I had one,' he bravely admitted. 'Singing barbershop is far too uncool for most girls my age.'

'More fool them. I think you look very smart,' I said while. I stroked his black velvet tie. I could guess that his blood was now pumping to the places where pleasure hangs out. This wasn't flirting, it was flirticide. But the poor boy wasn't finished yet.

'Just because I haven't got a girlfriend it doesn't mean

I can't sing a song for you,' he said. 'What's your name?' Nice work Brian.

'It's Annie,' I said. I could guess what was coming. He held a swift conference with the three other barber shop choirs and there followed a brief moment of pitch-setting before they burst into an impromptu version of *Annie's Song* by John Denver.

'You fill up my senses…' –and it would have done, except that at that moment Justin, my boyfriend, came back from his call of nature. He didn't look too thrilled to find sixteen men apparently singing a song in my honour.

'What the fuck?' he said, smiling through gritted teeth.

'They're singing my song,' I explained, unnecessarily.

'I dread to think what you had to do to make them sing it,' he said with a sneer.

When they'd finished, of course I had to applaud it, for it would have been rude not to have thanked them, wouldn't it? Unless of course your name was Justin.

'You can have your nerds,' sneered Justin. 'You're welcome to them. And all the others you like to mess around with too,' he railed. He got up to leave.

'No, please don't go,' I begged. Call me superficial, but he had such nice white teeth, and a body to sigh for.

'How can I possibly compete with such a choir full of dorks?' he said as his parting shot. Suddenly his teeth didn't seem to shine as brightly as before.

'Oh dear, we seem to have upset your boyfriend,' said Brian, with a smile.

'Ex-boyfriend. Another one bites the dust,' I sighed,

before knocking back a whole glass of Chardonnay in two sips. 'You see, I have this habit of frightening men off.'

'I would have thought it would have been exactly the opposite,' he sweetly replied.

'Do you know what? You're cute.'

For once I wasn't flirting. I actually meant what I'd just said. How weird was that? The more innocent he appeared, the more I desired him. Yet surely this was against the flirting code – it was only supposed to be a game, after all. It was time to put up my defenses. Yet instead, I only went and confessed to him.

'You see, I'm a flirt. There I've admitted it. And it drives boyfriends to distraction. But it really shouldn't, should it? I'm only having harmless fun, and I would never ever cheat on a boyfriend, however much I lusted after someone else.'

I wished I hadn't added that last phrase. I was now certain that I would frighten him off, having already admitted that I was only talking to him for the sake of fun.

'If you were my girlfriend I would let you flirt with whoever you wanted. What's the big deal?'

Well he would say that, wouldn't he? Although I did begin to notice that he'd got rather attractive eyes, not to mention eminently kissable lips.

'Ah, you say that now, but when push comes to shove, I doubt you could handle it, sweetheart. It wouldn't be fair on you.'

'Let me be the judge of that,' he came back at me undeterred. 'So why not allow me take you on a date and see if I can be true to my word? And no restrictions need apply. If you see some guy you want to flirt with, then be my guest – Just as long as you're there at the end of the evening for me to deliver you to your door.'

'And you genuinely think you could deal with me and my wicked ways?'

'I can handle it. Asking you to stop flirting would be the same as asking me to give up barber shop singing. They're just hobbies, but important nevertheless.'

'Get your coat on, you've pulled,' I said to him as we walked arm in arm into the cool evening air. And he had strong arms, so important in a man, don't you think?

Sometimes a girl just has to do what a girl has to do, regardless that I had broken the golden rule of flirting by dating one of my victims. In my world, flirting was strictly for sport. And Brian was a million miles from my usual type. When it came to boyfriends – as opposed to men to flirt with – I'd always dreamt of dating smart, rich, fit guys who, when they weren't down the gym honing their beautifully-toned bodies were out making huge amounts of money to lavish on their honeys, namely me. Who cared what was in their heads just as long as they had an extremely large bank account. And a personality would be nice too, although never top of my list of priorities – I had girlfriends and gay men for that.

My girlfriends often said I should have set my sights higher, and that I was dating below my league. Maybe it was because I believed that I was average too, and this was about as good as it was going to get for me.

So here was spectacle-wearing Brian – not exactly an Adonis, was he? Arguably well below average in the dating league, but what a personality, yet as geeky as they come. He had little experience of women from what he'd told me, but he was blessed with a Grade A in great conversation and the art of listening. And above all, he was happy for me to be myself – a flirt – or so he claimed. Therefore, I needed to put him to the test.

I had thought of reining myself in on our first proper date, as a mark of respect for his role as new boyfriend in chief. But then it struck me that I should start as I mean to carry on, for if he couldn't handle my position as Queen of the Cockteasers from day one, there would be absolutely no point in us continuing to a second date. And after all, Brian being happy for me to remain a flirt was his unique selling point, and what had prompted me to become his girl in the first place.

He couldn't have got it more right than by taking me to a bijou little Italian restaurant where there were bound to be gorgeous waiters in tight black trousers highlighting their pert provocative bottoms who would only be too happy to take the bait and flirt.

Brian and I spent the first course talking contentedly with one another. I listened to him getting lyrical about his barber shop singing, and then his study of psychology and his hopes of becoming a personal counsellor, helping people to unravel their problems.

'Maybe you'll be able to sort me out, and cure me of my addiction to flirting,' I suggested.

'I wouldn't try, even if I could. It's who you are.'

We were getting on so well that I hardly noticed any of the waiters as they poured wine into our glasses and wielded their unfeasibly phallic pepper mills over our respective pizzas.

Brian was a good listener too, as befits a trainee counsellor, as he patiently concentrated on some of my more familiar gripes about my mother, my job and the stupidity of men. Plus, he had lovely grey eyes, although I still couldn't stop wondering why he hadn't got a girlfriend, as I really didn't buy all that stuff about barber shop guys being a turn off for girls. Maybe he had other issues.

Then he made his excuses and retreated to the gents'.

'You use that with such confidence,' I teased the handsome waiter.

'I could teach you how to handle it, if you like?'

'Be my guest,' I coyly replied. My eyes darted towards his pants and back again.

He moved around to stand behind me, his crotch brushing against the back of my head as he leant forward to assist me in his masterclass in how to fondle a pepper mill. 'You grip this here,' he advised me, just as Brian emerged from the restroom door to see the waiter entwined around me.

Now this would totally test the limits of Brian's ability to endure my flirting.

'Ooooh! It is very impressive. I'm not sure I can get my hand around it,' I said, loud enough for Brian to hear from where he stood a couple of tables away, hiding behind a pillar.

'The ladies never complain,' Luigi replied. 'Now twist here, gently back and forward. Not so hard.'

'But that's the way I like it,' I said, glad to see Brian's amazed yet far from outraged expression. I would even go as far as to say that he looked amused.

'Is there anything else I can get you?' said the waiter.

'Laters baby,' I said, mimicking Anastasia in *Fifty Shades of Grey*. Luigi's departure gave Brian space to return.

'So what do you reckon?' I quizzed him.

'That was just plain wrong.' Ah – I knew he was too good to be true. 'But totally hilarious,' he added.

Result!

'I'm not normally that bad. All that leaning over me, it's usually more verbal than physical,' I said as a kind of apology.

'You had him wrapped around your little finger. Just as well you don't try and manipulate me like that.'

'I wouldn't want to do that to you Brian. With you, it's different.'

'And that's a good thing?'

'Let me show you,' I said, and later in my apartment, that's what I did.

He certainly lacked confidence, covering himself up until the last possible moment. In fact, he was passable naked – well, I'd seen much worse. Although it wasn't really his body I was craving – a little too skinny for my taste and nowhere near six feet tall, while he was clearly a stranger to the gym. I wanted Brian for who he was – a likeable, loveable guy, who was more than worthy of my attention. I counted myself lucky to have him in my bed.

OK, I can't say I was blown away by our lovemaking, except to say that the expression 'short and sweet' comes to mind. So what if he wasn't the greatest lover I'd ever known? What we had outside the bedroom was magnificent to behold, and what with my license to flirt with any man I wanted, I was about as happy as a girl can be. Or at least, that's what I believed at the time.

'Just look at you,' he once said upon discovering me sitting upon the knee of another mustachioed middle-aged banker. 'With that gorgeous long blond hair, your fabulous shapely legs, and those lovely pert boobs of yours – is it any wonder they can't resist you?'

'No, it's my conversation that fascinates them,' I protested.

And I genuinely believed that!

I had thought that having been given permission to flirt might somehow take the edge off the whole experience, but *au contraire*, it was as much fun as ever. It was kind of nice to know that I wasn't doing it at anybody's expense.

When Brian and I weren't working or studying, we spent most of our time going for long walks, watching scary movies and drinking cappuccino , while reading books by Donna Tartt and Conan Doyle respectively. In fact, he was the nearest thing I'd ever had to a perfect soulmate. I loved listening to his crazy theories, such as, why do rabbits breed so much? Because they are so darn cute with their white fluffy tails and smooth soft coats, how could they possibly resist one another? Or his pointless facts about the human body – for example, that your nose and ears continue growing after you've died. 'If I live to be one hundred years old I'll be just one giant nose and two great ears on legs,' he joked.

But he wasn't just some annoying nerd busy boring me with fascinating but ultimately useless facts. With his instinctive empathy and his knowledge of human psychology he would listen to me talking deep into the night about my weird attitude to men, and why I liked to tease them so.

'It's all about power, you see. Because men see you as a sex object, first you feel the need to remind them that you are as much about brains as you are about beauty. It's your way of striking back.'

'Oh *puhlees*, Brian! I'm nothing special,' I replied. 'I haven't got what it takes to be one of those willowy tall models on the catwalk, the type all the magazines go so crazy for. I'm just a dwarf with breasts, and that's why guys want to make fun of me.'

'Well that's where you could be wrong,' said Brian. He poured another cup of black coffee into our cups to help keep us awake. 'You are what men really want. Real guys don't go for all that skinny stuff – that's just for other women and gay guys to look at. You've got to have more belief in yourself. You're a perfect ten.'

'You really think so?'

'I know so.'

At that moment I really wanted Brian to be the father of my kids – and I didn't even want kids. Trouble was, he wasn't that convincing in the sack department, and that surely had to be a requirement of the job. I guess that whole staying up late talking habit we'd gotten into had as much to do with trying to avoid having ultimately disappointing sex as wanting to discover the meaning of life. Not that we didn't occasionally hit upon some real gems of modern Western thought as we talked the night away.

'So tell me, Professor Clever Clogs, how could I be cured of flirting?'

'Well it might have started as a defence mechanism,' he opined, 'but it's finished up as an end in itself, when it really should just be about being a means to an end.'

'It's late, and that's deep,' I sighed.

'Let me put it another way. I think you need to follow a flirt right through to its natural conclusion, from beginning to end, if you're ever going to cure yourself of your flirting addiction.'

'Well I flirted with you, and then I had sex with you, and now we're together.'

'That's a start, I'll admit, and a good start, at least from my point of view. But – and it really hurts me to say it – you need to set your sights on a man who's more worth laying, not some middle-aged guy who's over-grateful to have your attention, or a geeky young fellow like me who's more friend than lover. What you need, Miss Annie

O'Brien, is to flirt to fruition and to have some deeply meaningless, wild sex with a young fit guy who's hung like a horse and goes like a train. And only then will you be free of your addiction to flirting.'

'Why so?'

'Because flirting has become your defence mechanism of choice. It's preventing you from moving on and having sex with the kind of guy you really want.'

He wasn't majoring in human psychology for nothing.

'And what happens once that's done?'

'You have some more deeply meaningless wild sex with another young fit guy who's hung like a horse, and so it goes on until you find Mr Right.'

'So where do you fit in to all this?' I had to ask.

'I'll probably be back singing barbershop.' He pulled a face. 'It's time to get real.'

I would have none of it, and I gave him the best blow job of his life so far to confirm it. I even put a self-imposed ban on my flirting, at least when I was out with Brian. I would show him that I didn't need to devote the next few years of my life to a series of meaningless sexual exploits with gorgeous young men. I wanted to be unhappy, like everybody else.

Trouble is, all of this giving up on flirting had started to affect me in a strange and troublesome way. It was sending me quite loopy, forgetting appointments and generally becoming disconnected from the world, as if I was orbiting in outer space and looking down at my life from another planet.

It didn't take long for Brian to notice it – he never missed a trick, that boy. He begged me to resume flirting as before, and even to take it to the next level if the right guy could be found.

'OK, maybe I might reward myself with the most meaningless of flirts, just to get my head right,' I promised him, as we walked towards Penn Station on our way back to Boston after a day out in New York.

'But only if it's a hot young guy. No geeks or safe middle-aged gents allowed, and then we will see what you're really made of.'

'You're weird Brian. You're not one of these guys who gets off on his girlfriend having sex with other men?' I enquired as we disembarked from the bus.

'Most definitely not. It will break my heart, but I fear I'm holding you back and I can no longer stand in the way of your progress. You're the worst case of arrested development I've ever encountered.'

Looking back, he really must have loved me so much that he was willing to let me move on by allowing me to go with another guy. Or maybe he didn't love me enough.

OK – here's the thing – once in a while on the flirting scene along comes a guy who really tests your resolve to stick at level one, tempting you to the point of endurance not to take your encounter to the next stage. And Jake was one such guy.

I thought I recognized him as he came sauntering down the train corridor with his devil-may-care attitude. He was a top professional basketball player who appeared regularly in the New England press and on local and even national TV.

'Is there anybody sitting here?' he asked.

'No, it's free,' I lied. Brian was away on a mission to buy some drinks from the catering car.

'Are you going all the way?' he asked.

'Depends on who it's with.' I paused for the shock to sink in, and then continued, 'unless you're referring to something else completely.'

At that he took a long hard look at me.

'And what have we got here?' he said smiling. He began to laugh. 'You and me would make a great couple together – me six foot six inches, and you, barely five feet tall.'

'Getting a bit ahead of ourselves, aren't we?'

He sniggered, like a man who was used to dictating the pace.

'I'm actually over five feet,' I proclaimed defiantly. 'So there, Mr Six Foot Tall.'

'Don't forget the six inches.'

'That's never going to happen,' I said, and immediately wished I hadn't.

'Well we're all the same lying down.' He laughed suggestively.

'That's never going to happen either,' I said swinging back from wanton woman to virtuous girl.

'I've brought you a latte,' said Brian, unintentionally interrupting our flirting match.

'Oh thanks babe. Jake meet Brian, he's my…'

'Gay friend,' said Brian. 'Nice eye candy. Enjoy, girlfriend,' he said, giving me a high five with the limpest of hands and then disappearing towards another car, God bless him. He was so far from gay, with his nerdy spectacles and corduroy jacket, but Jake hardly noticed him anyway. If truth be told, he only had eyes for me. And I should have only had eyes for him. He was everything a girl could possibly want in a man, at least on a purely animal level.

He had more muscles than the Atlantic Ocean, while exuding more testosterone than a heavy metal, guitar-playing, firefighting lumberjack, not forgetting his lazy crooked smile and those ever-important strong muscular arms.

And yet still I couldn't get Brian out of my mind. Sure, he wasn't going to win any prizes when it came to looks or performance in bed. Sex is so overrated anyway, and Brian allowed me to flirt to my heart's content, which turned me on more than a locker room of athletes any day.

When I looked into Jake's eyes it was as if I was about to fall head first into a swirling whirlpool which threatened to sweep me away, but I didn't care. I would flirt and run, just as soon as the train arrived at our mutual destination, and no numbers, addresses or bodily fluids would ever be exchanged.

'What you need is a slow hand,' I advised him.

'You know me so well,' he leered back.

'For your back, given your height and your occupation, you must experience a lot of stress on the lumbar region, especially for up to forty-eight hours after a game.'

'Are you a doctor? You don't look like a doctor, more of a naughty nurse. I would pay money to see you in that white uniform of yours.'

'I didn't realise there were still men like you around – from the Stone Age.'

'Oh you mean a real man – one who can take you to places you would never imagine possible.'

'I've already got my own transport, thank you very much. I'm a mobile physical therapist. I treat people at their homes.'

'Impressive,' he mumbled. 'Then why not visit my door with your bag of magic sponges to see if you can magic my aches and pains away?'

The train rattled through the New England countryside, hugging the abundantly pretty coastline on its way towards its eventual destination of Boston, home of the Celtic Tigers, where Jake played basketball, in defence.

'I don't think that would be a good idea, do you?'

'You mean you wouldn't be able to control yourself once you were tempted by my fit lean body in the raw,' he said, elongating that final word to an almost obscene length.

'You are so unreconstructed,' I railed, producing a Kindle from my purse to signal that I was now past flirting, let alone anything else.

'No. You've got me wrong,' he said, waving his hands to try to divert me from reading my tablet. 'You're pretty and smart too. That's a bonus.'

'So having a brain ought to mean I should be plain?'

'You disprove the rule.'

'Well it's a shame you don't disprove the rule that all sportsmen keep their brains in their pants.'

'Where else would you want them?' he said, in between bursts of laughter, 'when there's somebody as hot as you sitting so close to a guy like me. They couldn't be better placed.'

Although he said the most dreadful and inappropriate things, I kind of liked him for his honesty and his irreverence. So what kind of person did that make me?

'You may not realise it, but you are sitting next to a fully qualified physical therapist, and the only interest I could ever have in your body would be professional,' I admonished him.

'Well, if it makes you happy,' he said before going off into a rant that can only be described as unreconstructed. 'I just don't get it. Why a babe as attractive as you would want to bother with education and training, and doing a job when you've got the means to bleed a guy dry with the way you look is beyond me.'

I shouldn't have dignified his comment with a reply, but I did.

'So that's what you think of women is it? Prostitutes, and all the rest.'

For a moment he looked genuinely hurt.

'Am I that Neanderthal? So let me prove you wrong. How about I book you for treatment to my back to see if you can get it fixed?'

'It's a deal,' I said without hesitation. I was beginning to wonder whether I'd been outwitted by the guy with the brains in his pants.

'And can I just remind you that as a qualified physio I will only ever see your body as a problem to be cured.'

'That's what the last one said,' he replied with a smirk as the train drew into Boston Central Station. I gave him my business card and a highly formal handshake before linking up again with Brian, who was waiting for me outside on the platform.

'Did you give him hell?' Brian enquired as we made our way to the T Line.

'I think he might have got the better of me,' I reluctantly replied. Brian's face fell.

Back in my apartment we talked about all kinds of other stuff before the conversation inevitably turned back to the herd of elephants which were stampeding around the room.

'So you're going to see Jake again?' Brian enquired.

'Only in a professional sense. He's an athlete with a bad back, and I'm going to treat him.'

'I see,' said Brian in a crestfallen kind of way. 'You don't have to do it if you don't want to. After all, we're happy as we are, aren't we?'

'Happier than I've ever been, Brian.'

'You see I was thinking, while I was pretending to be

gay, alone in the other car, if you're happy and I'm happy, then why shouldn't we carry on as we are, and to hell with your arrested development and other crackpot theories. You have to grab happiness where you find it.'

'We're not getting a touch jealous, are we Brian?'

'Not about flirting – no way – but I wouldn't be able to hang around, knowing you've been with another guy.'

And I was pleased to hear it. I didn't want Brian giving up without a fight. It wasn't natural, and I didn't want to lose him either. So I walked over to him and gestured for him to stand up, where we held each other tightly in one another's arms.

'This visit to Jake will be purely professional,' I said, comforting him.

'I suppose he is rather hot, isn't he? It's always so hard for a straight guy to know what kind of man turns a woman on.'

'I'll cancel his appointment then.'

'No, don't do that. I would hate you to think I don't trust you.'

I suppose I should have been honest with him and told him that there was a type of man who was so darn gorgeous that no woman could ever completely guarantee her fidelity – think Brad Pitt, George Clooney, and Jake. I suppose some things are best left unsaid.

It wasn't until I turned up outside Jake's high class apartment that I sensed just how difficult it was going to be for me to resist him. Of course, I put on my finest performance of assured professionalism at first, suitably dressed in my white smock and cotton trousers. I instructed him to take a warm shower while I got the tools of my trade together alongside the couch where he was about to lie semi-naked. And when he emerged from the bathroom, the water dripping from his abundantly masculine frame, a white cotton towel draped around his waist, I feared for the outcome. Still, I commanded him to make himself decent and put on his Calvin Kleins at once – it felt like I should have been awarded virgin of the month for that alone. He lay on the couch face down and I probed and prodded his lower back.

'Please don't get the wrong idea,' I said as I slipped his Calvin Kleins a little lower to gain access to his upper buttocks – for good medical reasons, I might add.

He sighed.

'Does that hurt?' I said, putting extra pressure on the tops of his buttocks.

'Only in a so-good kind of way,' he replied.

'I don't think you're taking this seriously,' I protested. Trouble was, neither was I. I hitched up his shorts to hide his deliciously peachy bottom, afraid I might crack at any moment and take a big bite of it.

'Over on to your back, please,' I ordered him.

Now when giving guys massages it's not uncommon to see a little expansion down below when it's time to turn over. It's what's known as an occupational hazard, and often to put the guy's minds at rest, I would use a phrase like 'it's nothing I haven't seen before'. But when Jake turned over I couldn't in all conscience say such a thing.

It was up there with the greats, but I wasn't about to let him know it. I wasn't going to say anything that would inflate his ego further. Besides, I had my professional standards to think of. I could be struck off the list of registered physical therapists for doing what I really wanted to do with him.

I tried so hard to resist, thinking about boring stuff like the need to relax his muscles in iced water for thirty minutes after games, but nothing could deter me.

'Do you know what? I've done enough talking these last few years. Now all I want is action,' I said. Then I placed my hand on his manly chest and pinned him forcefully to the ground.

'Whoa, steady girl!' he squealed.

'Now you're going to find out what it feels like to get well and truly fucked,' I taunted him. I think this was what they call hate sex. But I didn't hate him enough to refrain from giving him oral.

'How could you resist?' he boasted.

'I've known better,' I said in between taking gulps of air.

'Oh I don't doubt it.'

'You have no idea!'

'Didn't your momma used to tell you not to talk with your mouth full?' he hit back.

'Oh you think I haven't heard that one before, you not-so-clever dick.'

'Is all this included in my sport therapy package, or does it cost extra?'

'I'll charge you double if you fail to satisfy me. So, are you man enough Jake?' I said, embracing my inner whore.

'I should throw you out of my bed,' he said. He leant over and removed my sexless smock and next the decidedly sexy Victoria's Secret red demi bra I'd worn underneath, just in case anything should happen. I don't suppose you also want to read about how he separated me from my matching Cutout Cheeky Panty with his teeth. Or first used his finger and then his tongue to light the blue touch paper of my body to ignite in a firestorm of pleasure, managing to make me feel worthless and priceless at the same time.

'Fuck me like the fucking selfish bastard you really are,' I challenged him.

'Not much of a stretch,' he joked.

But it was for me, as he entered my amazed pussy. It was all shock and awe going on down there as he drove himself deep inside me.

'Is that the best you can do?' I mocked him. I would never have said that to Brian.

'Shut it, bitch!' he replied. He gave an almighty thrust, using it like an exclamation mark.

'You fucking cock!' I yelled at him.

True, I hated almost everything he stood for as he towered above me, impressive in his magnitude, pummelling me so hard that I could barely distinguish between what was pleasure and what was pain.

'Take that, you whore!' he replied. He was such an old-fashioned, romantic fool. It was unadulterated, dirty, loveless sex. Why had I never experienced anything as thrilling as this before? Too much flirting, I guess.

Of course, there was a high price to pay for it, because when I finally realised what I'd been missing over the years it marked the end of me and Brian. I'd tried to let him down lightly but I didn't really need to – he knew as soon as I walked through the door that I had taken the ultimate cure to flirting by getting well and truly ravished by an alpha male kind of guy. Brian had been right all along, yet to say that I missed him would have been an understatement. However, being friends wasn't an option for him.

I carried on seeing Jake for a while, and we fucked each other senseless until we got bored with one another, because there was never anything worth talking about once we'd finished our workout in the bedroom. And after three years of working my way through some of the greatest and most gorgeous sports stars in the land – my job rather conveniently lending itself to hooking up with a string of athletes to lie for – I began to wonder what was going to happen to me once I stepped off this sexual carousel of thrilling yet meaningless sex. As my girlfriends began to marry off one by one, I despaired at being the last single girl of my group. I even tried to magic up meaningful relationships with totally unsuitable hot guys who were always as brilliant in the sack as they were useless at commitment. How I missed being addicted to plain old flirting. The cure was certainly worse than the illness.

After about three years of living like this, I was invited to the wedding of another of my girlfriends, with me in tow to another fine specimen of masculinity, Darren, a quarterback with the New England Patriots – as wow a guy as you could ever desire yet seriously wanting from the neck up. As we sat through the couple's declarations of love, yours truly with a fixed grin on my face, trying to disguise my intense envy, up stepped a barbershop quartet to serenade them. Of course, this instantly reminded me of Brian. And at that moment I decided that should one of them, by some incredibly freaky coincidence of fate, *be* Brian, I would beg him to have me back. And do you know what? There he was, singing *I Just Called To Say I Love You* along with three other guys, who understandably all faded from view. I loved that song.

Just as they got to the closing cha cha cha bit I stood up and slowly walked towards him. You should have seen the look on his face.

'Brian,' I said getting down on one knee, kneeling directly in front of him. 'Will you marry me?'

There was an audible gasp from the crowd, and a couple of screams, one of which came from him.

'Only if you agree never to stop flirting,' he at first replied.

'Whatever,' I said.

'Well then, sure I will,' he answered.

Up went a great cheer as he held me in his strong arms. I like that in a man.

So did we live happily ever after? Pretty much, and as

the song goes, I'm true to him in my way. We did all the things we used to love doing together, mostly staying up into the early hours talking nonsense, but not so much that we didn't find time to raise three great kids, two boys and a girl.

And have I carried on flirting with other men? Well of course I have – it's my antidote to having meaningless yet thrilling sex with hot young athletes. Yes, I'm still working part-time as a physical therapist, now for the legendary Boston Red Sox. And maybe occasionally if I have to supply a little extra TLC to one of my needier athletes, it becomes incumbent upon me to flirt extravagantly when out with Brian – just so he doesn't become the slightest bit suspicious about where my professional boundaries might lie.

But please don't get me wrong – most of the time I'm only too grateful just to know that some of these really hot guys even think twice about wanting to ravish me. That's usually more than enough to keep the fires burning down below, but just once in a while I need to be reminded what it is to have shallow but breathtaking sex with a super stud, if only to convince myself how grateful I should be to have Brian.

And I have to admit that such a thing happened only last night. So if you will forgive me, I need to get flirting with this guy at the bar, just to reassure Brian that everything is OK between us when he arrives in about three minutes' time.

Would I consider leaving Brian for a beautiful Adonis? Never in a million years, because I love that guy from the bottom of my cheating heart.

And would I ever give up flirting?

'Can I get you another drink sir?' said the bartender to the smart-looking stranger sitting next to me at the bar.

'No thank you. I've already been intoxicated by this beautiful young lady's smile.'

Here we go.

I think you've got your answer. I guess you better leave me to it.

AS IF!

At the risk of appearing indelicate, no matter how you dress it up, there's always something irresistibly funny about a wiener – unless of course you're a man, and it's attached to you.

Not that I'm proud of it, as in every other aspect of my life I'm the last person to laugh at the less fortunate. I vote Democrat, I give regularly to charity and I have even been known to attend church. I'm a caring person – but if I encounter one of those seriously small ones I instantly become challenged by a whole cocktail of emotions.

Let me introduce you to one I met earlier, back in my dating days, when I was dressed to excite, so full of anticipation and expectation about the cute boy who worked in the hardware store, until he finally got me alone and revealed something so unfortunate I wanted to scream, *what the hell do you expect me to do with that?*

First, there was the heartbreaking disappointment – all undressed and nowhere to go –then anger that he'd got the nerve to think that his tiny little whatsit would somehow satisfy my needs, and finally, the stifled laughter, because small ones are innately and utterly funny. They are absolute proof that God is a girl, and she has a great sense of humor.

And however much you try and reassure the guy 'it's fine' (to be said in a dopey, dreamy faraway voice, with head tilted to one side, not forgetting to assume the concerned face), up comes the irresistible urge to laugh out loud, all thoughts of sex now dispensed with, trying to reassure him through suppressed giggles that, of course size doesn't matter. It's just a complete coincidence that you've suddenly developed a dreadful migraine in between the howls of laughter, and could we meet again some time after hell has frozen over.

Personally, I blame Mother Nature – she's a woman too, of course – for doing everything she can to deter us from making out with men who don't quite make the cut sizewise, and if that includes making us helpless with laughter, so be it.

You see, I reckon it's in our genes to be amused by what's not in guys' jeans. I can only apologize for it, especially as I haven't always been your typical size queen. When I first met my husband it wasn't his penis that particularly impressed me, nor even the size of his bank account. It was his easy laid-back charm, like nothing much mattered, except for me. So I'm not a totally bad person, am I?

Plus, I was crazy for him too, loving all of his little ways, although you would never have described him as passionate. And seeing as we've been talking full frontal here, he was standard sizewise, yet for some reason he seemed to think he'd been exceptionally well blessed in the pants department. He was as proud of his male member as Justin Bieber, sometimes waving it while dancing around in the bedroom for my delectation when in truth, it didn't impress me that much.

'You're such a lucky woman, Adrienne,' he would say as he pranced around our bed naked, flaunting himself. I wouldn't have minded if he had known what to do with it, but looking back on our love life, in spite of all this ridiculous showing off, he never actually had the snap crackle pop you would expect from a young man who'd lucked out by marrying me, the Blow Job Queen of 1988 (it was written on the Guys Rest Room Wall of Fairfax County High – embarrassing, I know).

I digress.

So, I gently tried to correct his somewhat exaggerated view of his male member, as I didn't want to hurt him, nor did I want to admit that I'd previously witnessed more than my fair share in my single years, giving me the perfect right to know the difference between that will do (his) and that will do nicely (unfortunately not his).

He even took to suggesting in public that he was hung like a horse. 'No wonder my wife's always got a smile on her face', he announced to astonished friends seated around the steak house dining table.

'Whoa! Too much information', said Barry, who'd booked the table.

Why, tell us more', said his over-dressed, over-made up wife.

I guess I should have pretended to be amused, and dismissed it as a joke, but how I hated seeing all those women in the room, most of them under the influence of too much booze, eyeing him lasciviously in the mistaken belief that he was God's gift to women. I should have spoken up there and then, and let the truth be known.

Finally, after attending another friend's barbecue when he'd been busy bigging himself up, my patience finally snapped, although I waited until we were driving back home in the car before I spoke my mind.

'Stop going on about your blessed penis, especially when we're out in company. I refuse to put up with it any more. How do you think it makes me feel? Humiliated, that's how,' I told him. 'It's not right, accurate or appropriate. And you know what they say, pride comes before a fall.'

I had no idea what I meant at the time, and I guess, neither did he.

I needed a plan.

In the meantime, still I tried to make the best of it – after all, marriage isn't just about sex, is it? He was my friend, my confidant, and for a guy, he never complained about accompanying me shopping either. Unusually for a man, he had great taste in women's fashion – he could have been a personal shopper instead of the slightly boring management consultant he turned out to be.

Whatever passion there might have been soon became a distant memory as I evolved into your standard desperate housewife, all needs taken care of, except one. Much as I secretly fantasized about a hot, eighteen-year-old gardener coming to water my roses, he never showed up. Not that I'd totally lost the art of catching a man's eye, although I didn't realise it at the time. I was lucky enough to possess long flowing blond hair, piercing blue eyes, and most notably, a heaven-sent set of *au naturel* boobs with surgical uplift, which everyone admired except my husband. He didn't even want to talk to my chest, let alone my eyes. Not that I wanted him to start banging on about his exceptional whatsit again – not if I had anything to do with it – and even he didn't seem to believe in its grandeur any more. But a normal sex life would have been nice. Something was obviously wrong, so I decided it was time to send in the cavalry, my sexiest lingerie – a black Dream Angels floral lace bustier with silk stockings and suspenders.

'You like, you naughty man?' I purred in a phony French accent as I paraded in front of him where he lay in our bed. I know, embarrassing. 'But this isn't for you, oh no, it's for Tony (our neighbor) and all you will be able to do is watch him fuck me while you go play with yourself.'

Now before you go judging, the idea of me being ravished by another man had been his ultimate fantasy for as long as I could remember, and these days, it was just about the only thing that was guaranteed to turn him on. Personally, Tony wasn't my particular cup of coffee, but if it kept Mike happy in the bedroom, then it had to be done.

Anyway, I pulled back the covers expecting to see him reasonably enlarged. In fact I couldn't see anything at all.

'Mike – your thingy! Where's it gone?'

I couldn't believe it. Here I was, a middle-aged housewife working my way through the three-step program for dealing with an absurdly small penis.

First I had to navigate disappointment. 'I was so looking forward to it,' I said like a spoilt child.

'But I've still got the urge – thinking of you fucking Tony,' he pleaded with me.

'Mike, what on earth do you expect me to do with that?' I guess that was stage two, anger. 'I've seen more meat in a vegetarian restaurant.' Stage three – hilarity. I was unable to suppress the laughter any more. 'Since when did this happen? And it's erect too,' I said fumbling under the bedclothes to feel his tiny dingaling.

Quick – it was time to adopt the caring pose, head to one side, not forgetting to assume the sympathetic face.

'Poor you,' I said stroking his forehead.

'I was hoping you wouldn't notice.'

I thought about making a joke about my eyesight not

being that bad, but I resisted.

'Much as I feel your pain – and you know how I completely respect you Mike – you can't really expect me to let you, er… have me with that.'

'And what would you say if I did?'

'Is it in yet?'

I let him dwell on that for a moment before letting rip with a hurricane of my own laughter. Yes, I know it's not cool to laugh at your own jokes.

'What's going to become of us?' he bleated. 'It was our pride and joy.'

Well, yours, maybe!

'Come on sweetheart – we can work this out.' Yes, I actually said that.

'And I really don't want you to have sex with Tony. That's just fantasy.'

'Then we've got to get it fixed, Mike.'

'So how am I supposed to do that?' he asked, a hint of desperation in his voice.

'By going to see the penis doctor. Come on, let nursey have a look at it.' I whipped away the bedclothes.

'Omigod, a second belly button. How cute,' I said. His unaroused organ looked like a baby bird asleep in its nest. But in spite of all my jokes, I did care, of course, because that's the kind of wife I was.

'So why didn't you mention it before?'

'It's not something you want to talk about, especially when you've got a surname like mine.'

OK, let's get the laughing out the way now. His name

is Mike Weiner. So no surprise that he'd become so obsessed about his size, and no wonder I preferred to use my maiden name, Monroe.

'And how long has it been like this?'

'Ever since I had this dream,' he replied. 'It was so real that it appears to have come true.'

As if! But I decided to engage with his world anyway.

'What on earth could have happened in this dream that's caused you to lose your manhood?' I said.

'I'll tell you, but only if you promise not to laugh.'

I nodded.

'I was visited by this fairy...'

I laughed.

'You promised!'

'You were visited by a fairy in your dream,' I said plainly and without cynicism, trying to get him back to the matter in question.

'But she wasn't your typical fairy – much too sexy for that – bouffant blond hair, skyscraper heels, an eye-catching cleavage, bright red lipstick.'

'That must have been nice for you.'

'Not at all! Because there I was, standing in front of her, naked, covering my shame with my hands.'

'One hand would have been plenty, love.'

He sighed. 'This fairy told me to stand up straight and put my arms down by my side, which I did, causing her to giggle. "I am here to grant you one wish," she said, "and from what I've just seen, I don't think it's going to be for world peace".'

'And this was a dream?'

'Yes, although I'd never felt so ashamed, especially considering my surname. I always thought I'd been well blessed in that department, but upon seeing her reaction… plus, where's the harm in wanting a little more?'

'So what went wrong?'

'I told her I wanted to be bigger down below. "Now there's a surprise," she replied. "You want a bigger dick – spit it out honey!" "If you please," I replied. "That's better," said the fairy. "It's at this point that I am supposed to say, your wish is my command, but I have to inform you that I am in fact a bad fairy, and whatever you ask for, I shall do in reverse, and then some. So she waved her magic wand, reciting the phrase, "neither a grower or a shower shall you ever be. Adieu".

'I awoke in a state of terror. I put my hand on my dick to be greeted by the smallest one imaginable. Plus, my balls had shrunk too, and that's not fair, because they weren't even part of the deal.'

'But it was only a dream, Mike.'

'It felt real enough to me, and look!'

I couldn't disagree. Neither of us was imagining the vanishing act his wang doodle had performed.

'It was never going to win any awards, sweetheart, but now…'

I saw the pained expression on his face.

'I've lost my mojo,' he said, and started blubbing.

'You've lost more than that, honey,' I said trying to make light of it. A further cascade of tears. I was only trying to brighten the mood. Sometimes I don't know why I bother.

'What we need is some professional help.' I told him. 'We'll go and see the doc, but no talk of fairies and dreams, if you please. We don't want them locking you up.'

Our first port of call was our family practitioner, who breezily proclaimed, 'I'm sure you've got nothing to worry about'. That was until he got close up and medical with Mike.

'If I hadn't seen it, I wouldn't have believed it,' he said as he made notes, which didn't exactly boost Mike's confidence. So he was referred to a specialist, who worryingly for Mike turned out to be a woman. He insisted on me accompanying him to the examination to give him moral support – big mistake. When I saw the gorgeous cockologist with the mascara eyes, bleach-blonde hair and the slash of red lipstick, I instantly recognized her as one of us. And however much she tried to hide her true self by means of her professional demeanor and long, unpronounceable medical phrases, plus those reassuring words 'Don't worry Mr Weiner, I've seen it all before' – I just knew she was going to burst into laughter.

'She looks like the bad fairy in my dream,' Mike said.

'I told you not to mention that nonsense again,' I cautioned him.

'Extraordinary,' was her first reaction, her lips quivering and her voice quavering. 'Well there's a first. I can safely say I've never seen anything like it before. Unless you count those tiny little cocktail sausages on sale at my local delicatessen'. Then we both lost our self-control, but still Mike failed to get the joke.

After he'd been prodded and poked and sneered at by countless more experts, we eventually received the ultimate diagnosis. Apparently, I was married to a one in a million guy who had a previously unknown condition, now to be named in his honor, called Weiner's Syndrome. So, I was hitched to the one and only incredible shrinking penis man, and there was nothing much they could do about it, except take photographs and display them in medical textbooks for students to laugh at.

I begged him not to give up – not just for my sake, but for his self-esteem too, which had taken one hell of a battering thanks partly to my occasional weakness in finding what should have been his pride and joy laugh-out-loud funny.

'What about a penis extension?' Mike asked the white-coated cockologist at our next consultation, more in desperation than hope.

'Ah, bless!' she replied. 'It's really not worth the bother. Just like your wife in the bedroom, the surgeon needs something to work with, and when it comes to an implant you haven't got nearly enough to make that viable.'

He sat transfixed as she smiled condescendingly at him.

'Neither a grower nor a shower shall you ever be,' she added, giving him a teasing flutter of her eyelash extensions which would not have been out of place had she been inviting him into her bed.

'That's exactly what the bad fairy said,' said Mike. 'It's her!'

'You'll have to forgive him. It's all the stress he's been going through,' I said.

'I totally understand. So many men with penis-related concerns claim to have met me some place else. It must be some kind of hysteria. And as for you, Mrs Weiner,' she said giving me a knowing wink, 'let me introduce you to the most amazing sex toys.' She handed me a brochure and whispered into my ear, 'although a hot young stud bearing an eight-inch dick is more what this particular doctor would prescribe.'

Who would have thought it, from a doctor?

Still I tried to reassure Mike when we got home.

'There's always oral,' I began encouraging him.

'Not one of my favorite things,' he replied, like Julie Andrews in reverse. I knew his heart had never been in it, let alone his tongue.

'But you could become real handy with a vibrator, and I will always be there to give you a helping hand,' I said. I really wanted to say, a helping thumb and little finger instead.

It was as if I just couldn't stop myself. My hand was shaking with repressed laughter, but I took a photo of his funny little thing at his request, because he'd been asked to send an image to the Boston Institute of Urology.

You'd think he would have been devastated by his medical condition, but after the initial shock had sunk in he began to take it in his stride. He was saying that we were past all that nonsense anyway, and announced that he was moving into the next bedroom so he could enjoy a good night's sleep.

So what was I supposed to do? As far as I was concerned I was still just about too young, and hopefully desirable enough to shut up shop. Thank heavens for friends who encouraged me to believe that I wasn't totally past it.

First I told my best buddy, Molly, over the kitchen table while Mike was safely out of earshot listening to his Elton John records. She grimaced, straining to adopt the sympathetic pose. Then she assumed the caring face, head tilted to one side, but I could still see the corners of her mouth twitching.

'Aw poor Mike. And poor you too,' she said in a faltering voice. "Maybe you could persuade him to wear a strap-on.'

Of course, we both erupted in hilarity at the thought of it, just as he walked back into the kitchen. He was pretty certain I guess that it was his shortcomings which were shaking our tits with laughter, poor love.

I was required to go through the whole procedure again two days later when Molly arranged a gathering of all my female friends in a downtown bar. It was a sight to behold, seeing them all struggling to repress their laughter as they religiously observed the rules of the three-step response. Finally, I could bear it no longer.

'Get a load of that,' I said flashing my iPhone at them to share the incriminating evidence of his reduced circumstances. It was wrong, I know, but isn't that really what they wanted to see? There was a momentary collective gasp, then laughter was unleashed – gales of it – and I joined in too. You see, I couldn't help myself – it's what women are programmed to do.

Then after we had laughed ourselves senseless they marched me down to the nearest 24-hour sex aids shop and stocked me up with every kind of electronic gizmo known to woman. My Rampant Rabbit certainly helped me through some very dark nights. But it's not the same as the real thing, is it? Actually, it's better – who says you can't improve on nature?

And yet still I longed for a real one. I was becoming almost obsessive about guys' packages, and my eyes were darting down towards eligible men's pants at totally inappropriate moments. I had become the female version of all those men who had ever stared at my chest, but I was staring at their crotches instead. It seemed like I had become a total Size Queen overnight. Even a trip to a male strip show, arranged by my friends – purely for my benefit, of course – failed to satisfy my hunger. In fact, if anything, it made it worse, because there was only the briefest flash of what I had come to see before they would rush off stage to protect their modesty.

'Much too tasteful,' I informed my friends, as ironically we drank cocktails at the bar. And surprisingly, they agreed, especially considering they weren't the one living with the incredible shrinking penis man. Some of their husbands were incredibly well endowed – or so they claimed – yet even they had desired to see another man's cock, if only to reassure them how lucky they were.

Maybe that's what first got me thinking about the idea of a high-end venue where classy women with healthy desires, like us, could come to gaze at awe-inspiring cocks attached to fabulous young male bodies for the ultimate ladies' night out. Is that really so shocking? That's not to say we don't enjoy lots of other manly bits too – take your pick – such as pert bottoms, broad backs, muscular chests, rippling abs, strong arms, and the rarest of all, the ability to listen. But you don't have to be married to the incredible shrinking penis man to admit to being fascinated, intrigued and entertained by the male member. If we're lucky, they grow big and bold in response to us – how incredible is that? Yet admit to being bewitched by dick in polite company and you will never be invited back to the PTA again.

So that's when I first discovered there could be a gap in the market.

All these thoughts and more were going through my head when the doorbell rang announcing that I was about to be saved. And we're not talking Jehovah's Witnesses here. There he stood, sex-on-legs gorgeous, a body to lie for, lightly muscular, wavy jet black hair, soulful brown eyes, a jawline that could have lifted girders, a pumped-up chest, and best of all he was wearing tight blue jeans – and when I say tight I could see straight away that he wasn't suffering from incredible shrinking penis syndrome. If anything, had I not noticed the slightest hint of expansion down there? I was sure I had.

'Hello. I'm here to repair your TV,' he had said, for the third time.

'Oh sure,' I said, my eyes speeding back upwards again, only too happy to see that he had locked on to my boobs. I dipped down below for another sneaky look, only to discover that he appeared to have grown already. Considering how desperate I was, you can only imagine how that made me feel. 'Moist' would do it.

'Nice jeans,' I mumbled incoherently.

'Nice blouse,' he gallantly replied. Then, just like that, he stepped over the threshold, took me in his arms and kissed me forcefully on the lips. Naturally I opened my mouth to welcome him in. And as he held me tighter I felt the hardness of his expanding cock. A real man at last, and I had been denied one for so long. So what else could I do, except kneel down and partake of it, enjoying its abundant beauty and power.

It seemed to go on forever, the infinite cock, and I licked it while simultaneously holding his massive balls, one resting on each hand. Up and down I played with them, almost comical I know, until he knelt down alongside me and unbuttoned my blouse, then deftly unclipped my bra, with not a fumble in sight. He buried his face in my chest, sucking each nipple in turn, tingling my tits off as he created this most incredible connection between my breasts and my pussy of a kind I'd never experienced before.

He then followed the pleasure trail down to my love button, teasing and tormenting it with his super-sensational tongue and sending sexual shock waves through me. Was it possible for a woman to die of having too much pleasure? Well if so, I was within an orgasm of my life. He didn't seem to want to stop licking me, yet although I was enjoying his ingenious tongue more than cut diamonds, or Gucci handbags or saving the planet, how I wanted him to enter me.

'Fuck me!' I begged of him, and he duly did what he was told. I like that in a man. He took me so totally that he nearly went up to the hilt of his gigantic sex sword – gently backwards and forwards it went, until I screamed out loud in pleasure, cloaked in pain. It was big, remember, and his thrusts came ever harder and quicker. If I had been a gaming machine, I would have been all lit up and paying out fortunes.

'I love your lovely cock, your beautiful balls, and you've got nice jeans too!' I cried out somewhat insanely.

'And I love your fabulous tits, your heavenly pussy and that sexy silk blouse of yours,' he replied. I was particularly glad of it. How I loved that blouse!

On and on he went, rigorously and remorselessly and relentlessly pounding and pleasuring and penetrating me – hoo-wee, how I adored it. Orgasms like little love bombs were exploding inside of me.

'I want you to come,' I begged of him, and he obeyed me again, like the well-behaved sex machine he so obviously was. Jets of warm juice gushed out of his gigantic unprotected cock deep inside me, and I could feel every drop. How I wanted to bathe in it, like Cleopatra in her bath of milk. OK, so I'm getting a bit carried away here, and don't go lecturing me about unprotected sex, he hadn't made love in ages, and I was later to find out why.

We lay on the living room floor together for a matter of minutes in an embarrassed silence until I got up and fetched us a couple of fluffy white dressing gowns and we flopped on to the sofa, neither of us quite sure what to say or do next. Yet I didn't feel guilty or ashamed. After all, I was only following doctor's orders. I must remember to send that white coated cockologist a thank-you card.

'What's your name?' I asked him.

Talking can be so much more intimate than sex.

'Dick,' he replied.

'Now why doesn't that surprise me?' I giggled. 'I'm Adrienne.'

'Nice name, Adrienne,' he whispered into my ear.

'Are you married?' I dared to ask him next.

'Separated,' he replied. 'My wife ran off with her lover, and took our kids with her.'

How could anyone possibly want to leave this guy?

'What the hell is wrong with her? Unless she's a lesbian.'

'Got it in one,' he said.

'Omigod! And how did that make you feel?'

'Well, put it like this – you're the first woman I've had sex with in over six months.'

'Are you serious?'

'I'm not some man whore who has sex with any woman who will let him, if that's what you're thinking.'

'You've got the body for it,' I teased him, 'although I'm kind of glad to hear it. So why me?' I just had to ask him.

'I felt the need in you.'

'You mean, you thought "she's desperate, I'm in luck here".'

'You don't have such a great opinion of yourself, do you? Well you should,' he said, turning his face towards me and looking me directly in the eyes. 'I just had this feeling that there goes a fabulously sexy woman who has been shamefully neglected by somebody close to her, and seeing the need in you helped me to accept the need in me. Does that make any sense at all?'

Men are so full of shit.

'Totally,' I replied.

'You see, until I met you, I'd never felt less like a man in my life.'

'Trust me Dick, you're the most man I've ever known,' I said placing my hand on his cock. It began to swell to extraordinary proportions again, so divinely, incredibly, amazingly responsive to my touch.

'She hated me being this big,' he said, nodding towards it.

'You were wasted on her, Dick,' I said stroking it and staring provocatively into his eyes. 'Do you fancy getting dirty in the shower?'

And he did. On the way I took a diversion via the kitchen to grab a familiar household implement to confirm his magnificence for my records.

'Eight and a half incredible inches on the dickter scale,' I declared, waving the tape measure in the air as if I had been announcing the dimensions of a prize vegetable at a county fair. And as for girth, it should have won awards there too.

We held each other in silent union for a while until I couldn't resist stroking his provocative bottom. That was all it took to set him off yet again. He was beyond insatiable, taking me from behind in our bathroom, and then I climbed aboard him – ride him cowboy! – plus who needs Pilates when you can work on your inner core by being on top of a guy who's that well blessed?

'Oh God, you're incredible!' I said, leading him back to our sofa again after another strenuous sex workout. 'The vibrator would never have been invented if every guy was like you.'

He gave a modest laugh and adjusted his white fluffy dressing gown.

'You're the first man I've slept with in 25 years of marriage,' I explained to him.

'So you're recently separated too?'

'No. I still live with my husband, although our sex life has long since left home.'

You should have seen the look on his face when I informed him that Mike was out of town having his dick and balls displayed to over 50 medical experts studying incredible shrinking penis syndrome. But he didn't laugh, even when I gave him the full story, unlike girls I'd previously told – male solidarity, I guess.

'I feel for you,' was his first response, 'and I pity your husband too, although he can't really expect you not to look elsewhere, can he?'

Well, I wasn't going to argue with him, was I? Yet I needed to keep him talking, for in my heart of hearts I realised that what had just passed between us was destined to be a beautiful one off. He was alpha male plus, unlike any man I'd ever been with, and I desperately didn't want him to leave, fearing that I would never see him again once he'd walked out of that door.

'I'd better go and fix your TV,' he sighed. 'I've a got an ex-wife and two kids to support.'

'I guess you have to work all the hours God sends,' I said, making small talk as we both got dressed, ready to address the dreary reality of everyday life again.

'That's for sure. I'm trying to hold down three jobs,' he said, hoisting his pants up to his waist. 'That's why I only get to see my kids a couple of hours every month. Some kind of dad I am.'

And then it struck me. I thought once again about that all-male review I'd seen the other night, and how not one of those guys came close to my Dick.

'There must be an easier way for you to earn a living,' I said, adjusting my top. Who could be better than Dick to turn women on? He was every female's fantasy of fantastic fucking proportions. Of course I would have preferred to have kept him all to myself – I would simply loan him out for hire as a totally naked dancer and then get him back at the end of the day, as I would be his manager. Purely a business relationship, you understand, but if anything more came of it, that would be claimed as a perk of the job.

'You're going to hate this,' I said, holding his hand as if to give him strength to deal with my impending inappropriate question, 'but have you ever thought of becoming a male stripper?'

'An astronaut, a rock star, a train driver even, but a guy who takes his clothes off in front of hundreds of drunken, screaming women, surprisingly, no.'

'You'd drive 'em wild,' I said, brushing my hand across his crotch. 'And I could negotiate you the best rates and would only book you into upmarket venues. You'd be strictly high end.'

Sure, it sounded insane, but I would have suggested just about anything to keep a connection between Dick and me, and although this crazy idea had been forged in the white heat of desperation there was a logic to it. I could really see a business opportunity developing. I visualized branding and logos, plus maybe a whole roster of dancers performing under the banner of Adrienne Monroe Artists (my maiden name). The guarantee of breathtaking male beauty, and the absolute certainty of everything being revealed – and if it was less than seven inches you would get your money back. We would call it 'The Great Tape Measure Challenge'. My star performer would always be Dick.

He seemed less than enthusiastic about the idea as yet.

'What the hell would my kids think about their dad flaunting himself on stage in his birthday suit?'

'They would think trips to Disneyland, designer sneakers, X Boxes, and much more importantly of all, more quality time with their dad, because you would only have to work a couple of evenings a week to earn three times what you are earning now.'

I'd hit a soft spot. I even persuaded him to get all his clothes back on – and who would have thought I'd be doing that? – and dig out an old track by James Brown called 'Sex Machine'.

'Let's see what you can do with this,' I said clapping my hands to bring him to attention. 'Just dance,' I commanded him (I wasn't always this bossy). It's time for you to bump and grind.' And again he obeyed. He danced a touch furtively at first, so I joined in with him, until he relaxed a little.

'Now thrust,' I instructed Dick. 'And thrust again.' He was already good enough for me to leave him to dance alone. 'And thrust… and thrust encore… now remove that shirt, slowly and seductively. Now shake your booty in my face.'

I was now sitting down, watching his every move.

'Now remove pants.' I could see he needed assistance as I encouraged him to grow. 'Now take off those Calvin Kleins,' I purred at him, and off they came.

'Omigod, that ought to be illegal,' I said, marvelling at what was revealed.

I don't think my husband was anywhere near as impressed when two seconds later he opened the living room door to see Dick standing there in all his gigantic cock-and-balls glory.

'What the fuck?' he spluttered.

'I know what you're thinking Mike, but it's really not what it looks like,' I protested before quickly regaining my composure, 'although you couldn't really blame me if it was'. That was just about enough to put him on the back foot. 'You see, what we have here is a prime financial investment, and you, my hard-working husband, can now be confirmed as Assistant to the Manager – that's me – of Adrienne Monroe Artists. Mike, say hello to Dick.'

'Pleased to meet you,' he said disbelievingly, looking from dick to Dick and finally shaking the latter's hand.

'If you say so,' Dick replied. He began climbing hastily back into his pants, and then turned to me wearing an expression of astonishment. *You cannot be serious!* He mouthed to me.

'Well, what do you think, Mike?' I asked

'He's, er... big, isn't he?'

'Big? He's going to be massive. He's my surprise package from me to you. It started on that girls' night out, you see. We went to an all-male review.'

'I see.'

Thankfully, by now Dick appeared mildly amused by my quick thinking, and he agreed to return for further rehearsals the next day. At least I had created a weird kind of connection between us, knowing that he would be back.

The next job was to persuade Mike to make an appointment at the Bank to negotiate a loan.

'And make sure to ask for Cindy Baker, and tell her she can inspect her investment in the flesh,' I said. 'I doubt she'll refuse.'

Mike was indeed successful in persuading Cindy to attend our impromptu show, and perhaps unsurprisingly, being a red-blooded woman, she agreed to loan us more or less whatever we wanted, subject to her getting her own private performance.

So that was how my global multi-million-dollar empire of celebrated male dancers began. This is supposed to be a story about business after all, but in my case, my business is also my pleasure. At first of course I was totally dependent on Dick, whom we whipped into shape in two weeks flat in time for his debut at a Bachelorette party for a society wedding, where he went down a storm.

Of course he was nervous, but I was there to give him a helping hand – it was a tough job but somebody had to do it – and he didn't disappoint the bride-to-be either, although her wedding night must have felt like a real letdown after she had seen Dick's magnificence.

And in spite of all the female attention he received, which I had to accept as just being part of his job description, our relationship grew ever stronger, and closer. Yes, we continued to have plenty of wild sex – he was like Viagra on legs – yet in between all the traveling and the live appearances we really began to connect.

While I took care of business – he seemed really grateful for my managerial expertise – I could also sense he really cared for me. Whenever the negotiations with the club owners and theatre managers began to wear me down, he would enfold his strong arms around me. I felt safe with him, as if I had found the one, and while I never actually admitted to Mike that my relationship with Dick went beyond business, I didn't really have to.

I encouraged Mike to become involved with the business, although I worried about the effect being around so many well-hung guys might have upon him. I needn't have been concerned – it was like he'd finally found his vocation. He even enthusiastically participated in judging the auditions for my first ever troupe, the Cockendales, my answer to the Chippendales. We guaranteed that absolutely everything would be revealed, and boy, were they big. They sold out wherever they played. I at first employed a risquée comedienne as their show opener, but I felt I needed something else – a complete contrast to the group if you will – when I inadvertently caught sight of my naked husband coming out of the bathroom. He'd been working out at the gym, I suspect in a vain effort to rebuild our relationship – he was still in denial about his sexuality back then. I just couldn't resist a giggling at the sight of him, which inspired me to come up with a truly outrageous suggestion.

'Mike, do you remember how you used to enjoy waving your pride and joy around in the bedroom, and how it annoyed me so much, to the point where it sent me insane with anger? Well not any more!'

'Why torture me? How could I possibly forget? If only I could do that now.'

'But you can, because weirdly, at long last you've now got something special to celebrate.'

'Don't you mean humiliate?'

'Let's agree on entertain. What if you were to open the Cockendales show with a solo strip routine? Reckon the ladies would find you totally hilarious."

'What, laughing at my expense?'

'More like at their expense, because they'd be the ones paying. So if I find the contrast between your newly-honed body and your cockette funny, then why wouldn't 500 slightly pissed-up women think the same way?'

'No way! I've got my pride to think of.'

But when I reminded him that most of my girlfriends, all of my male dancers, the check-out team at the local superstore, the guys at the gas station and Cindy at the bank all knew about his little problem, he reluctantly began to consider it.

'Well, what have I got to lose?' he finally replied.

'Very little indeed,' I agreed, and for the first time in a long while he gave me the hint of a smile back. He was beginning to get the joke.

And that was the start of his recovery, mentally speaking. Mike threw himself into developing a hilarious routine devised by our newly-appointed choreographer, Tamsin Tonioli, who got him to strut his stuff in a sexy, no limits kind of way. He danced with wild abandon, like a man who had reason to be proud of what nature had given him, until he whipped off his artificially enhanced posing pouch to reveal... well, virtually nothing.

'I haven't laughed so much in years,' said Tamsin, blissed out by their rehearsals, and the audiences loved the finished product too. Women stood in line to have their photos taken with Mike and giggle hysterically at his unfortunate predicament. I'd never known him happier. Here was a natural show-off who really loved being on stage – so much better than being restricted to dancing naked around our bedroom to an unappreciative audience of one – and because the crowd could sense he was having a genuinely great time up there they felt comfortable about teasing him back. If only his glamorous cock doc could see him now.

So, I just couldn't resist inviting her to a venue later on during the tour, which didn't exactly endear me to Mike. While she loved every minute of it, Mike seemed highly uncomfortable when she sashayed into his dressing room after the show to present him with a bouquet of red roses. And I thought it would be a nice surprise for him, because I'm a caring person, above all.

'Oh no, not the bad fairy,' he said, still traumatized by his dream. 'Are you two in this together?' He had clearly gone out of his mind through seeing her again, but it was too late to get her out of there.

'You darling little person. Well I couldn't call you a man after seeing that, could I?' she said. She caught my eye and we set one another off laughing. We'd become a great team, his therapist and me, two feisty women on a shared mission to make the world a better place. All that prancing around all those years ago, waving it about in our marital bedroom, when he only had something that was at best average, then humiliating me in public. I might be a caring person, but how could I possibly let that go unpunished?

I watched him look at us suspiciously. Was he beginning to realise that we'd worked together ever since I'd warned him that pride comes before a fall?

'What a divine performance. But never forget that you owe it all to me, darling', said his therapist. 'But that was the real star of the show." She pointed down at his posing pouch.

Well if his act could make a cock therapist laugh, what psychological harm could it possibly be doing him, putting him on stage in reduced circumstances for the amusement of hundreds of partying women? I'd never felt so vindicated in my life.

Thankfully Mike's routine was not only hilarious but lucrative, and as the money started rolling in we expanded further, starting with the Frat Boys, an 18 to 21-year-old male dance troupe aimed primarily at the college circuit, but moms loved them as well. Meanwhile, Dick's career went from strength to strength; the only downside was being away from him while I was developing other acts. True, I did enjoy the responsibility of looking after all of the other guys and trying to resolve their various issues – who says men can't be divas? – and first night nerves can play havoc with a young man's cock.

All in an evening's work, but when I got home to Dick he was the only man who mattered, and we continued to enjoy mad, passionate sex at every opportunity. And while he became something of a celebrity after appearing on *The View*, Dick never became too big for his posing pouch.

Some of the gigs were truly incredible though, like being flown first class to London for a certain 'hush hush' royal girls' night in to celebrate the birthday of Pippa, sister of Kate, the future Queen of England. And sure, I wasn't exactly thrilled when I found out that she'd licked whipped cream off him, inch by inch – but it was his job, after all, just as occasionally having to be hands on with the Frat Boys was mine. What Dick and I had together was indestructible, regardless of our strange lifestyle, promoting and celebrating the male form, all for the delectation of women.

Our success as AMA Artists has of course been widely reported, especially the grandeur and opulence of our Hollywood mansion where Dick and I now hang out, while my ex-husband Mike has moved into a much smaller property in a far less fashionable part of town with none other than our old neighbor Tony masquerading as his personal assistant – and I mean personal.

You see, Mike had never really wanted me to sleep with Tony after all. He'd been living out his fantasy through me, and it was my husband, not me, who wanted to be banged by the guy next door. Sex isn't straightforward or simple, is it? I was glad for him – such a shame that he'd had to suffer incredible shrinking penis syndrome after having allegedly been visited by a bad fairy in order to discover his true sexual orientation. There must be easier ways of finding out. I guess he'd always been that way inclined, long before his penis shrank in the wash.

'Hey girlfriend,' I said, patting him on his cute little bottom in between stores while doing some serious shopping on Rodeo Drive. 'I couldn't be happier for you and Tony.'

'Well, we got there in the end,' he graciously observed.

'I'm sorry I wasn't always as sympathetic as I should have been, what with you and your bad fairy. How could I not find that funny?'

'I think you were in cahoots with that… creature.'

'Now if you carry on talking like that you'll have to go back on your meds again'.

'I don't think you're quite as caring as you sometimes think you are,' he suggested.

'But it hasn't always been easy for me either, struggling to keep a straight face. How easy do you think that's been?'

'I rest my case.'

What a diva he'd become! Such a blessing to know that he now had Tony to mop up all the really serious stuff, given there weren't enough hours in the day for me to fix his life.

Thank heavens for gay men.

Looking back, how could I have missed the signs? I

guess his love of retail therapy and passion for Elton John should have made me suspicious. And although he came out to me, and those close to him, I insisted that he should keep his sexuality secret for professional reasons, as I realised that a small dick is far funnier for women if they believe its owner could have designs on them. In fact, he totally embraced his new-found fame. Women adored teasing him wherever he went, while his website, Mock Mike's Weiner, got more hits than Game of Thrones. So maybe he'd had the last laugh after all, having made some serious money from his burgeoning career. I graciously allowed him as much as ten per cent of all profits from his shows, merchandise, and social media spin-offs, while the remaining ninety per cent was shared between his therapist and me. Our little secret, if you don't mind. We also trademarked his dick, although we retained one hundred per cent on that little honey. Just carry on shaking your money maker, Mike, because soon we'll have made enough for Dick to hang up his posing pouch for good, and I'll have him all to myself at last.

So that leaves Dick and me, as happy as two people together could possibly be. On our days away from the stresses and strains of our business, we would walk hand in hand by the ocean, the sun on our skin and the breeze in our hair. And in the evening we might catch a burlesque show – we both shared a love of watching beautiful girls in figure-hugging costumes dancing to sweet, sexy songs as it provided a welcome relief from our more blatant male dance reviews. Plus, girls are so much easier on the eye, aren't they?

Also, as promised, Dick found more time for his kids, as his ex-wife, Nicole, became ever more cooperative, almost certainly helped by being on the receiving end of his extremely generous divorce settlement. And much to Dick's surprise, I kind of liked her, proving that it was possible for two potentially rival women to bond, initially through our mutual love of the music of Alison Krauss.

His children meanwhile slowly began to let their wicked stepmother into their lives, although reluctantly at first, until I was eventually accompanying Todd and Jennifer on trips with their father to Disneyland and the Universal Studios Tour. Maybe I'd never realised how rewarding children's company can be, providing it comes in short measures, as we'd never been blessed with children in our first marriage.

Then, blissfully, Dick and I would occasionally get to spend a night in together – just the two of us. And one magical evening as we held hands on our veranda overlooking the Hollywood Hills, drinking pink champagne, he reminded me of that first time he came knocking at my door, and how our lives had changed beyond recognition since that wondrous, fateful day.

After gently squeezing my hands he wrapped his strong, masculine arms around me, making me feel safer and more protected than I'd ever done before. And then he rose to his feet, taking a step backwards. He cued in some sultry music and began gyrating his hips as he removed his pink Versace shirt, button by button, tormenting and teasing me, until he'd stripped right down to his gold lamé posing pouch.

This guy was never off duty, and here I was getting my own personal show. That would have been reward enough, but then he went down on one knee and removed a small black box with the word 'Cartier' inscribed upon it from his pouch.

He handed it to me.

I shrieked out loud.

'Will you do me the great honor of becoming my wife, Adrienne? He asked. What a stupid, beautiful question.

'Of course I will, Richard,' I replied, and he slipped the stunning solitaire platinum engagement ring onto my finger.

Suddenly, calling him Dick didn't quite cut it anymore. I would have loved him almost regardless of his male magnificence. So maybe, size nearly doesn't matter. And if I'd seen that slogan on a T-shirt, I'd have bought one, as would almost every woman I knew. Perhaps I'll start selling them through my clubs when I get back from our honeymoon.

For those of us lucky ladies who have an alpha male as husband or partner, maybe just the thought of it is enough to keep us feeling ultra-womanly, even when we are far away from home. But what really turns me on above all is that I now have a career with a flourishing business empire to call my own.

So when aspiring entrepreneurs such as you, the esteemed readers of *Women in Management* magazine, ask me for the secret of my success, my answer always remains the same. Think big, but never stop caring for those less fortunate, unless your first husband happens to get ideas above his station, and truly madly deeply offends you. Then simply magic up a bad fairy, and downsize him.

I can email you the spell.

A SUSPICIOUS MIND

Beware of the husband who after years of neglect starts buying you flowers for no apparent reason, or purchasing seats for shows you know he'd hate, or inviting you to join him for romantic meals for two in a restaurant in a way that is so not him. All this trying too hard can add up to only one thing – he's cheating on you.

Maybe you knew that anyway. Not that my husband hadn't strayed before. As a senator residing mostly in Washington DC, he was used to having attractive young women at his beck and call, and considering his great political role model was Bill Clinton, that's probably all you need to know about his take on the fidelity front. In fact, expecting him to remain faithful was like asking a lion to give up eating antelopes for Lent.

So Jeff was a serial cheat, while I chose to look the other way. Hardly the response of a heroic woman, I grant you. And having accepted the inevitable, then why hadn't I found consolation with another, seeing as I still had the power to turn heads if I put my mind to it? Maybe I didn't want to stoop to his level, or perhaps I hadn't found anybody so far who was worth all the bother of undertaking an affair. After all, it can be a messy business at the best of times, and as likely as not to end in tears.

Anyway, if he hadn't started bestowing gifts on me I'd have probably thought no more about it and dismissed it as just another one of his annoying little peccadilloes, while I filled my time with good works, doing what a senator's wife is supposed to do, helping the underprivileged in the community while he shagged his way around DC.

'I'm going to be late tonight,' Jeff said to me before leaving home that morning. Normally that would be a given.

'What's new?' I replied.

'I'm just trying to be a better husband by keeping you in the loop.'

Now where did he get that bull from?

'And what excuse do you have to wine and dine attractive young women this evening? Maybe I should join you.'

'You make it all sound so glamorous. Fact is, there's some Arab big guy in town who needs entertaining. It could be advantageous to helping the US maintain our influence there.'

'So you'll be taking him down to your favourite titty bar at the taxpayer's expense.'

'If that's what it takes. You might want to join us – most women are bi-curious aren't they, and you're more curious than most? It's what first drew me to you.'

How we enjoyed hurling insults at one another. It was our substitute for intimacy.

'In your dirty dreams,' I chided him.

They say power is a great aphrodisiac, with women far more likely to be fatally drawn towards a plain but powerful man than to a poor guy with great looks. And if he happens to have the whole package, then what's not to like? Just don't make the mistake of marrying one of these fine specimens of manhood, because you will never shake off the feeling of always being second best to the first big love of his life – himself.

If only I hadn't dated the boy most likely to succeed at High School. The boy who turned into Jeff.

I'd always wanted the best, probably why I strove so hard to be crowned Prom Queen, which of course I achieved. So what if I'd kissed the runner-up a little too enthusiastically? I was years ahead of Britney and Miley with their on-stage girl kissing. What wasn't to like? She was gorgeous, such a thrillingly lovely experience that I still sometimes think about it to this day. No more than a schoolgirl crush, I later realised, and a little bit of faux lesbianism never hurt a girl's chances of ensnaring a boy, did it?

Well, it certainly worked for Jeff, who sought me out after the great junior high girl kissing incident, desperate to meet this daring young woman who should have been kissing him.

But I digress. That didn't explain this sudden showering of attention and luxuries upon me by my husband some twenty-five years after we first made out. It unsettled me, making me fear that this latest girl of his could be so much more serious than any of the others. Could she possibly be the one, the one who would finally lure him away and dislodge me from my official position as the senator's wife?

I desperately didn't want to lose him – not because of status, or anything as shallow as that, but in my heart of hearts I truly loved him, and couldn't begin to contemplate that it wouldn't be me he would be coming home to at the end of the day. Does that make me no better than a carpet for him to walk on? Probably. So it was with a renewed sense of purpose and vigour that I finally decided to do something about it, to hire a detective – my very own private dick, if you will, a first for me as Jeff's PI had always been one of the most public in DC.

So no sooner had he left for Capitol Hill than I got googling, typing in 'private detective DC area'. Countless names and addresses popped up on the screen. I guess it should have been no surprise in a city populated by such an unhealthy proportion of sex-crazed politicians and their justifiably suspicious wives.

Having been raised on the works of Raymond Chandler, I was at first drawn to one of those world weary Phillip Marlow types, with me as the mysterious broad who sashays into his office exuding expensive perfume and an appealing degree of vulnerability, until I realised I was a touch too old for the role. And the world of private detection had moved on from those days, hadn't it? It was all bright young things with iPads and iPhones tracking down their prey without the need for face-to-face contact with clients.

And then out of the screen shone this young woman's face, a rose among the thorns of so many stereotypical males. It was her slogan that caught my eye: 'Let Me Be Your Dick'. A female private detective – why not? Who better to fight on behalf of a wronged woman than another female. She would feel my pain and understand my quest for revenge better than any man ever could.

The fresh-faced girl who stared out of the screen was appealing for me to send her all the lurid details of my husband's alleged infidelity by email. Doesn't anyone speak to anybody anymore? And I wasn't about to unleash sensitive details of Jeff's private life into the public domain without meeting this woman first. So I emailed telling her exactly why I felt the need to see her first. Call me old fashioned, but I had a political marriage to protect – I wasn't ready to go nuclear quite yet.

She had large blue eyes and wavy blond hair,

reminding me of the pretty one from Abba. I awaited her reply. When it came troubled me with its naiveté.

'Meetings are so last century,' she chided me. 'What's wrong with Skype?'

She might as well have been speaking a foreign language. Still, I persuaded her to meet me in her office, giving her a false name to protect myself from leaks to scandal sheets or trashy TV shows in the meantime.

So how should I dress for my appearance at Vanessa's office? That was her name by the way, Vanessa Bytheway. I wanted to make the right impression, just as I would when meeting any other professional, such as a doctor or lawyer, so the body fitted hound's-tooth wool jacket with black trousers would say everything that needed to be said about a woman who was clearly in control of her own destiny, albeit in need of a little help.

I never thought of myself as a celebrity in my own right – that was Jeff's job – despite the fact that my picture often appeared in glossy magazines or on TV entertainment shows and I usually arrived all glammed up at opulent charity events or glittering premieres, making me more famous than I really had the right to be. So upon meeting Vanessa maybe I shouldn't have been that surprised by her response.

'Omigod, it's you!' she blurted out. Hardly professional of her.

'If that's a problem, then I could go elsewhere.'

'No, please, sit down,' she said, trying to reassure me. I was sure I detected the hint of a blush on her face.

'I would have thought you would have been more than used to dealing with well-known faces in your particular trade,' I said.

'Please accept my apology. It's just that I wasn't expecting a celebrity.'

'I'm not a celebrity. I'm no more than the wife of a famous man.'

'But the very beautiful wife, whose picture I have seen in so many magazines, and I just love your style.'

'You're too kind,' I replied. I was unused to having my ego massaged after years of being married to Jeff.

'How can I help you?' Vanessa eventually asked me after we had engaged in a little meaningless social chit chat about the weather and the latest eviction from *Dancing With Stars*.

'First, I need to know that everything I say will be in the strictest confidence, because if this got out, there would be hell to pay.'

'Of course – that goes without saying, as you can see from my credentials and my membership of the United States Association of Private Investigators,' she said, pointing to the plaque on the wall.

'OK, here goes. I think my husband is messing about with another woman,' I somewhat clumsily blurted out. 'There, I've said it.'

To have seen Vanessa's reaction, you would have thought I had just said something quite hilarious. She was struggling most inappropriately to contain her laughter.

'What's so freakin' funny?' I had to ask, now totally

regretting my decision to hire this young woman as my private dick.

'Forgive me, this is most unprofessional,' she spluttered as I got up to leave the room. 'No, please don't go – it's just that your husband has the reputation of being one of the biggest players in DC, and I'd always assumed you must have known exactly what he was getting up to.'

'So I'm the laughing stock of Capitol Hill, am I?' I said. I was standing by the door now, determined to make my exit. 'I've never been so humiliated in my life.'

'Nobody is laughing at you, Mrs Keane. It's your husband who is the ridiculous one.'

'So it's pity people feel for me, is it? I think I'd sooner have their contempt,' I said, unaccountably returning to my chair.

'Can I fix you a drink?' Vanessa asked.

'I'll have a gin and tonic, and make it a large one,' I said, thinking how far this pastel shaded apartment with its Mediterranean chic was from the typical austere image of a private detective's office. 'Don't think I've been blissfully unaware of my husband's dalliances. What sort of sheltered world do you think I live in?'

She handed me a long glass, so I took a slug, then continued to explain why I had been drawn to seek out her services.

'Of course I've become used to enduring the latest in a long line of bimbos, but something told me this one is different.'

'How do you know?'

'A woman's intuition, I guess.'

'That's good enough for me.'

'Plus it's those typical telltale signs of him trying too hard to be loving and tender when he gets home, whereas with all his other affairs he would just carry on as if nothing had happened.'

'So this one's different?'

'It makes me think this girl is special to him in some way.' I lost my composure for a few seconds, unable to carry on.

'Take your time,' said Vanessa, gently placing her arm around my shoulder.

'I fear she could be the one who will break us up.'

'And maybe that would be for the best. But you must be the one to initiate proceedings. So let's find out who she is, shall we, and then you can decide what to do? After all, knowledge is power.'

I had now regained my confidence in Vanessa after our initial teething problems, and maybe the large gin and tonic had relaxed me a little more than I'd intended.

'So tell me, why the shocked reaction and the schoolgirl style blushing upon seeing me when we first met?' I asked.

'Well, you are pretty famous,' Vanessa said unconvincingly.

'No, there was something else going on.' I was sure of it.

'Well maybe there was, but we operate on a need to know basis in this office.'

'I need to know, so you can tell me.'

'Nothing much to report, except that on Sunday morning, I was lying in bed with my partner reading the weekend papers when we saw your picture in a magazine. You were looking hot.'

I didn't know what to say.

'And Sinead said, "if I was ever to have an affair with an older woman that's the kind of lady I'd go for". And I couldn't help but agree with her, although I felt a little jealous at the time.'

I didn't know how to react.

'I hope that wasn't too much of an admission, Mrs Keane. You must at least have thought about dating girls at some time in your life – most women do, even if they don't act on it. Take my mother – she's been fighting it for years by having a series of inappropriate relationships with the most macho of men, when I so know she would rather be dating women.'

'How on earth could you possibly know that?'

'She once confessed, after I first came out to her as being gay, that she used to have a massive passion for this girl at high school, and had always regretted not taking it to the next stage.'

'Oh, that's no more than the rose-tinted memory of a silly schoolgirl's obsession. We've all been there, and it's something most of us grow out of. After all, she eventually married and had you, didn't she?'

'Yes, but only after she finally kicked my father out did she admit to carrying out a search for this so-called girl of her dreams. She discovered that her secret sweetheart had only gone and married a man – as if it could have been anything else in those days – and from that day on she's devoted herself to a series of unreconstructed male chauvinists to try and take the pain away.'

'Well, that's more than I needed to know about your mother, but you can rest assured, I'm strictly a man's woman. You need have no doubt about it. I totally love my husband's manly accoutrements.'

Well – it was a very large gin and tonic.

'I would normally say "too much information", but as a private detective you can never have too many facts,' Vanessa said. We said our goodbyes, and she shook me warmly by the hand as I left.

I really liked this girl – apart from her typical lesbian obsession that deep down all of us must be gay like her. I felt I could trust her implicitly, but I awaited her call with a growing sense of unease.

Meanwhile Jeff had arranged another night out at a different musical, *Mamma Mia*, which I already knew he loathed, followed by a further slap-up meal, this time at a swanky Thai restaurant, my preferred type of cuisine although his least favourite in the world.

'What's this all about, Jeff?' I dared to ask while he nibbled cautiously on a spicy prawn cracker.

'Well, you like this kind of crap, don't you? Can't think why – it gives me gas.'

'You know what I mean. All these selfless gestures,

doing stuff together I know you hate. Are you trying to tell me something?'

'What is it with women? You do nice things for them, and they give you the third degree.'

'You make it sound like you're the wronged innocent party when I'm the one who's been cheated on for years. Don't think I won't get to the bottom of this.'

'Just sit back and enjoy the ride,' he said. I noticed he had that infuriating twinkle in his eye. Jeff still had the power to make me find him extraordinarily attractive in the most unlikely of places, although just why I slipped my hand under the tablecloth to touch him intimately I'll attempt to explain later. I started to stroke him, heedless of the ravishing Thai waitress who arrived just then to ask whether we'd enjoyed our meal. I sensed him stiffen exponentially as she approached.

'Oh, I come back later,' she said, sensing that something was going on.

'No, why not join us,' I dared to suggest, as she bent down to retrieve a napkin which had fallen on the floor. What was I thinking?

'Please forgive us. I think the champagne must have gone straight to our heads,' Jeff intervened.

'No, I like!'

'You want to touch?' I proposed as she accepted my offer on behalf of Jeff.

'You lucky lady,' she replied before running away while giggling.

I only tell you this sordid story to illustrate just how low I would go to hang on to him.

Perhaps it was my way of saying to him, so what do you need another woman for when you've already got a wild woman like me to initiate group sex in public places? You see, I'd never been one of those miserable wives who lose interest in sex the moment they ensnare their man. I was always seeking out new ways to entertain Jeff.

'Imagine if there'd been somebody with a smartphone filming the whole darn thing?' he challenged me in the car on the way home. 'You shouldn't have involved that Thai girl. What if she goes to the media?

'Why would she, when you gave her such a big tip?'

'Ha! Ha!' he sighed.

'I bet this new girlfriend of yours wouldn't have dared to do that,' I challenged him back.

'Can we talk about something else?'

Guilty as hell, I thought.

And that's exactly what I expected to hear from my private detective, Vanessa, when she called three days later. Her voice sounded more stressed that I'd previously remembered it.

'OK, shoot,' I said.

'I'd rather you visited the office so I can tell you in person,' she replied.

'Hang on a minute. I thought you were the one who believed in Twitter books and skypers, but now you're inviting me to have an old fashioned face-to-face conversation. Should I be concerned?'

'The truth will set you free,' was all she would reply.

I felt like I should be dressing in black for my second visit to Vanessa's office, marking as it almost certainly did the end of my relationship with Jeff. I should have been in mourning, yet still I lived in hope, praying that it was all some silly misunderstanding, or if not, then maybe this could be the beginning of a new life for me.

Precisely how new, I could never have guessed.

When I saw Vanessa in the flesh, it was as if all of her self-assurance had evaporated overnight, to be replaced by a nervous wreck of a young woman.

'I thought I was the one who was supposed to be stressed out,' I said as she fumbled around looking for the correct files for my case. I thought everything would have been on her computer.

'Do sit down,' she said, appearing distracted, as if she wasn't really in the room.

'Go on. Do your worst,' I challenged her.

So she did. She handed me a photograph of an unusually attractive middle-aged woman.

'Your husband is having an affair with this lady.'

I didn't hear much after that. It hit me like a punch, confirming all of my worst fears. Another one of his pretty young bimbos I could have coped with, but a mature woman meant only one thing; it must be serious. I studied the picture carefully, wondering whether there wasn't a spark of recognition of a person I'd known in a previous life.

'I think I might know her,' I said to Vanessa.

'Join the club. She's my mother.'

For once in my life I didn't know what to say. All I could think of was the phrase 'does not compute', which I had read in my brother's science fiction magazines as a child.

'Of course, this is most irregular,' Vanessa continued. 'You must understand I had no idea that my mother was carrying on with your husband. And I'm sure you will agree that I can't be held responsible for her behaviour. However, if you would like me to withdraw from the case I would totally understand.'

Her words were going over my head. What did I care if it was her mother who was being screwed by my cheating, lying husband? A weird coincidence, I grant you, but what frightened me the most was the knowledge that Jeff was hitting on a woman probably around my age when he already had a mature lady at home to fulfil that particular part of the age range.

'She is pretty,' I said.

'And out of her mind,' Vanessa replied. 'Sleeping with that sleazeball when she's not even straight.'

'That sleazeball happens to be my husband,' I reminded her.

'Sorry. I wasn't thinking,' Vanessa replied. 'You see I think that's why I probably shouldn't proceed with this case.'

'You're sure you haven't made a mistake?'

'How could I possibly mistake my own mother? She's the one who's been sleeping with your husband.'

'Then I suppose it must be one hell of a shock to you too. But I would like you to carry on with the case. The fact that it's your mother is neither here nor there to me. What matters is what we do next?'

Vanessa remained silent while I studied the image more thoroughly. I was becoming ever more certain that I'd met this woman before, maybe at a White House reception or some lesser Washington event. Hardly surprising really.

Vanessa then showed me a series of photographs showing Jeff and this woman together in various compromising situations. None of them were conclusive proof in their own right, but I just knew from the way they were looking at one another that the love light was shining in their eyes.

'I must meet her,' I said to Vanessa.

'I'm not sure that would be a good idea.'

'I need to tell her to keep her hands off my husband.'

'I've already done that, and she was having none of it. "It's my life, and I'll darn well do what I like," she told me.'

'I want her name and address please. And don't tell me you haven't got it. She's your mother, after all.'

So Vanessa scribbled down the details on a piece of paper, including the woman's name, Claire, and her cellphone number. 'Good luck, you'll need it,' was the only advice she would offer.

I decided that first I would confront Jeff and ask him what was he playing at and why he was willing to risk his marriage, his reputation, and his career for this woman. But I didn't get the chance. No sooner had he walked through the door on returning home than he dropped a bombshell of nuclear proportions.

'We must talk,' he said without further ado.

'No we mustn't,' I replied seeming to contradict my earlier plans, because I was dreading what was coming next.

'I'm leaving you,' he replied.

'No you're not,' I said clutching at him and straws.

'You know it's not right between us Jacqui, and it hasn't been for years.'

'Well let's work at it,' I begged of him.

'It's beyond repair.'

'There's somebody else, isn't there?'

'I'm afraid so.'

'I could have handled it if she'd been another one of your bimbos, but a woman of my age, and somebody I vaguely know. That's what really hurts.'

'So you've already heard? I didn't want to hurt you.'

'It's not too late to get yourself out of this mess, Jeff. You can go back to your old life, chasing bimbos and then coming home to me.'

I know. How I regretted saying that. That's what a combination of low self-esteem and total despair does for you.

'She's the one,' he finally admitted.

So I stormed out, and cried oceans in the bedroom, hating the way I had allowed myself to be humiliated and loathing every aspect of what I had become, all in the doubtful cause of staying together.

Well, if Jeff wasn't going to see sense, I was going to confront this Claire head on and force her to take her claws out of my man. Just then Dolly Parton came on the radio, singing *Jolene*. If it was good enough for Dolly to face up to her better-equipped love rival and beg her not to take her man, then I would do the same. Dolly rocks!

So with that song ringing in my ears I hightailed it down to Claire's apartment in the Shaw district of the city to plead with her. Trust her to live in such a hip neighbourhood with its trendy bars, restaurants and cafés that seemed to spring up from nowhere overnight.

But I didn't dress pathetic and sad, any more than Dolly would. I gave it the full works instead, just to remind my love rival that underneath this pathetic, pleading creature lay a real woman who was a perfect wife for her super, manly husband.

First I rang her doorbell, without reply. I later learnt that Jeff had told her to lay low should the media decide to call.

'I know you're in there,' I shouted out. I was started banging on her door as if I'd been trained by the drug squad.

And then Claire opened the door, and do you know what, she took my breath away.

'Oh, it's you,' she said, almost nonchalantly.

'Yes, it's me – the wife, in case you'd forgotten, the woman who's married to your lover.'

She was even more beautiful than I recalled her being at the School Prom, the girl I'd kissed – that was where I'd remembered her from, nearly thirty years ago. She was the woman time had forgotten. No wonder my husband found her totally irresistible.

'I suppose you want to talk,' she said, gesturing for me to enter her cool minimalist apartment. She obviously had great taste. I felt like saying, what's the point. I suddenly realised I had sent myself on a fool's errand. I was in awe of her, with her silky soft skin and the transcendent allure of her come-to-bed green eyes.

'So how's the Prom Queen?' she asked me.

I wanted to slap her face.

'Not as good as the runner-up,' I replied instead.

'That was a long time ago. But you're still looking great.'

'Please don't patronise me.'

'No I mean it. I was always in awe of you. You so deserved that title, and reckon I only got runner-up because I gave the organiser a blow job. Yuk!'

'You're kidding me! I always thought you were so pure – at least until we kissed.'

'Just a silly schoolgirl crush.'

'I couldn't agree more.'

'So I guess you're just going through the motions, pretending you're mad with me for screwing your husband.'

'I beg your pardon?'

'Well he has slept with just about every woman in

Washington who has a pulse. I thought it was some kind of agreement you had together.'

'No frigging way!' I shouted at her. 'How dare you be so casual about something that's so important to me!'

'Forgive me. I didn't know. I thought you'd be OK with it.'

'So this isn't some kind of warped revenge for missing out on being crowned Prom Queen?'

'Please give me some credit for having grown up!'

'But normally he only chases girls half his age.'

'I know. Well I can't say I wasn't flattered. But it's just the same old same old – simply another notch on his bedpost. I'm sorry if I hurt you.'

I sat there, my head in my hands. Didn't these lovers talk to one another?

'According to Jeff, he wants to leave me for you. Hasn't he told you yet?'

'Well he did say something along those lines last time we made out, but I told him not to be so silly, and thought no more of it.'

'But he's clearly besotted by you in a way he's never been with the others he's, er, made out with.'

'Then he's deluded.' She shook her head despairingly. 'I was only looking for another meaningless affair, and your husband was perfectly equipped for the job. It's the way I live my life, and my daughter hates me for it. She thinks it's because I'm running away from who I really am.'

'He's going to be devastated,' I said. 'But then why should I care?'

'Exactly! I'll phone him straight away to stop him making any dumb announcements to the press. Jeff is history as far as I'm concerned.'

I could have kissed her, so I did. And there was something about that kiss which told me our lives would never be the same again.

'That was, er, interesting,' I said to her.

'I still remember our first,' she replied.

'Me too. I wanted it to last forever.'

'But it was just a dumb schoolgirl crush.'

'My thoughts exactly.'

'So let's keep in touch,' I said as I backed out of the door.

'Yes, we can be friends, can't we? Just like we should have been all those years ago.'

I waved her goodbye and wandered back in the direction of home to do a little therapeutic shopping. I needed a totally new wardrobe for this next phase of my life. I would start with lingerie, and wondered what Claire would have bought for herself – something bold and provocative, I guessed, whereas I would be more understated. I didn't even think about what Jeff would have wanted me to wear.

Once my cheating husband had got over his distress at losing Claire, I was going to insist that he sorted his life out and ditched the bimbos, and then at long, long last, he could finally devote himself to me. Otherwise I would leave him too. He could take it or leave it.

Well – that's what I'd intended to say. The reality was

a little different. Sure, he was heartbroken about Claire – she'd already called him to say it was over between them – but he was mad with me for having gone to visit her and putting what he called 'a guilt' trip on her.

'You're the one who's trashed my one chance of happiness,' he said to me.

That really hurt.

'You're deluding yourself,' I hit back. 'She never wanted you for keeps. Anyway, her daughter reckons she's a lesbian.'

'Is that so? Well I hope you'll be very happy together.'

Just a schoolgirl crush, I reminded myself. I didn't say all that other stuff about him having to give up his bimbos. I needed to rebuild our trust first, and clearly it would take time.

While I was trying to get our relationship back on track I hooked up with Claire for a couple of enjoyable afternoons out in the park, or at the museum, or a little light shopping, just so we could get the whole thing with Jeff into perspective, or at least that's how it started.

Funny thing was, we never kissed again on meeting or saying goodbye. It was for the best, wasn't it? We didn't want our flourishing female friendship affected by such stuff. That was for foolish schoolgirls, and we were so far from that – two sophisticated women of the world, enjoying one another's company. What was wrong with that?

Mind you, Jeff wasn't exactly delighted when he found out that I'd been seeing Claire.

'So it's OK for you to see the bitch but I'm not allowed to. Is that it?'

'Yes Jeff,' I patiently explained. 'That's because I haven't been screwing her, unlike you. You even wanted to leave me for her, in case you forgot.'

'It seems darn strange that you want to be friends with the woman your husband fell in love with.'

I could have done without 'fell in love with'.

'I'm not asking you Jeff. Besides, she doesn't want to see you anymore, but she's happy to go out with me.'

Listen to me – I was starting to put him in his place. I wasn't some old piece of carpet to be walked over any more. Perhaps that's why he'd stopped chasing bimbos too.

But my friendship with Claire continued to go from strength to strength. Even Vanessa commented on it. She called to say that I'd been really good for her mother, especially now that she'd finally put the break on having affairs with unsuitable men.

'And I've heard your husband has stopped sleeping around. It's the talk of Washington,' said Vanessa, full of glee.

'I know, amazing!' I said, pretending to be excited about it. Trouble was, having tamed Jeff, and brought him back to me, I didn't really care anymore. It was like time had passed us by, and while he'd been dicking around I'd moved on to other things.

I thought about Claire and her lustrous blond hair, her luminous skin and her emerald eyes. How I loved being out with her, and we looked so good together. You could tell others were admiring us as we sashayed around town. And I looked better for it – she had been a tonic for me, making me look ten years younger, bringing me alive again with her wanton ways and her outrageous conversation.

'What first attracted you to Jeff?' she once asked me in a sedate little tea room.

'His voice. So sexy, or that's what I used to think.'

'And after you'd seen him naked?'

I blushed, and she laughed.

'Me too! Such a shame that it was attached to an even bigger dick!' she screamed with laughter, and people began to turn around and glower at us disapprovingly. But Claire didn't care. She was making me feel giddy.

The next day I waltzed into Victoria's Secret and bought her something bold and sensuous to mark our three-month anniversary of being best friends together. My heart was all a flutter as she answered the door of her apartment.

'I've got something for you,' I said as she undid the pink bow and ripped open the gift-wrapped parcel to reveal the shamelessly sensual black lace mesh teddy.

'Jacqui, that's an outrage,' she said, looking pleasantly surprised. 'You know me too well. Would you like me to wear it for you?'

'I would like nothing better,' I replied as she sashayed into her boudoir to begin her transformation from friend to wanton woman. I could hear her singing *Dress You Up In My Love*, and sensed a heavenly moistness between my legs.

Then she reappeared. She looked perfect.

'You're gorgeous,' I said, as we began to finish what we'd started thirty years ago. She took me in her arms and kissed me full on the lips, and it was more mesmerising than anything I'd ever encountered with Jeff, or any other man. Considering neither of us had ever gone this way before, everything happened as naturally as a flower opening up in spring.

'What do you want me to do?' I breathed, as I felt her soft fingers slipping down between my legs.

'Just do to me what you like doing to yourself, honey, and I'll do the same back in return and I reckon we should be OK.'

If that sounds a bit mechanical, trust me, it most certainly wasn't. It was smooth and soft, and moist and verdant as an orchard on a warm summer's day, with those lovely pink tipped fruits as an aperitif, and then her sex, tasting like the nectar of the goddesses, all salty and sour, with just a hint of peach.

Then Claire's tongue began to weave its sensual magic upon me, and I felt as if I was floating on a flying carpet, high above the cares of mundane existence. I hoped I tasted half as good as she did.

I cried out in delight. If I had been a musical instrument, you would have praised her for playing me like a maestro, compared to the clumsy guy who'd been trying to pluck me for the last thirty years. And that was only the overture.

We fell deeper in love as each day went by. When we

weren't buying beautiful clothes for each other in high end stores or going for romantic walks in the President's Park, we'd be staring moodily into one another's eyes in intimate restaurants.

'People will begin to talk,' I said, as we walked hand in hand in the fading daylight.

'Then let them,' Claire replied, ever the courageous one.

It was that time of year when leaves were beginning to fall. Claire fluttered gracefully down on to her knees in front of me, like a beautiful leaf herself, as if she was about to perform an outrageously erotic act in the park. But it was far more shocking than that.

'Jacqui Keane, will you do me the honour of becoming my wife?' she said. Then she presented me with a stunning Tiffany Soleste diamond engagement ring.

I only had to think once. I knew that after all these years, society would finally be ready to embrace our union, while unknown to us until now, our love had grown ever stronger as time had passed by.

'I will,' I replied without hesitation, and she placed the ring on my finger.

'And l want you to wear my ring too,' I said.

'You can be sure of it,' she replied, 'because we belong to one another, and the world needs to know it.'

We celebrated in a typical Claire way by getting outrageously drunk and then buying a bunch of sex toys, including a ridiculously large dildo. It doesn't get much more romantic than that.

'OK, I'll be Jeff first,' said Claire once we'd got back into the apartment, and we rolled around in laughter.

And talking of Jeff, I then had to pluck up courage to tell him about me and Claire.

'How did that happen?' he said in a disturbed whisper. 'I guess this is some kind of revenge for me wanting to leave you for her.'

'It's nothing to do with you Jeff. When I first went to see Claire my only thought was to beg her not to take my man. It was only over time that we began to rekindle our love.'

'So does this mean you're leaving me?'

'I'm afraid it does, darling. Claire has asked me to marry her, and I have said yes. Two people of the same sex can do that these days. I think you even voted for it in Congress.'

'Bitches from hell!' he yelled, banging his head against the living room wall. 'How could you do this to me?' I could see where he was coming from, and for the first time in years, I actually felt sorry for him.

'Honestly, it's for the best, hun,' I said putting my arm around his shoulder. 'She only ever wanted you for your body, whereas with me, it's kind of different.'

'I'm thrilled for you,' he replied sarcastically. 'Except, with all the women in the world, why did you have to hit on this one?'

I guess it had to be Claire, after I had fallen in love with her all those years ago at the School Prom. Strange that Jeff had helped bring us back together again.

'It's time for both of us to move on,' I counseled him.

'What if I promise to give up chasing young women, or any women for that matter? And you could still do whatever it is you do with the lovely Claire, as long as you come back to me at the end of the day.'

I should have told him to get real, except I too had known what it's like to be that desperate.

'You're not listening to me.'

'Or perhaps we could try three in a bed. That could be the best solution of all,' he said. That was more like the old Jeff.

'Now you're just being ridiculous,' I cautioned him.

It wasn't until after I'd left Jeff to move in with Claire that he finally accepted that this wasn't just a phase I was going through. He slowly began to pick up the pieces to start rebuilding his life, even making political capital out of the situation, publicly proclaiming that he'd been the one to suggest I should move in with a woman.

'That secured me two million more gay votes,' he later confirmed to me.

'Well, if you would like to win even more, how would you like to give me away at the wedding?' I asked him.

He considered the math.

'It would be a mistake not to,' he replied.

However, in spite of having become a born-again campaigner for gay rights, it wasn't too long before he got back into the saddle and started chasing bimbos again. And I was glad of it, because it meant he was in recovery, and starting to become his old self again. Of course I would have preferred him to have settled down with a woman who could have brought him genuine fulfilment than carry on being the oldest swinger in town. I truly wanted him to be as happy as Claire and me, but I had my doubts about whether he ever could.

What I didn't doubt was the way I felt about Claire, regardless that we had become one of the highest profile lesbian couples in the US. In many ways I still didn't feel gay – I was just oriented towards Claire, and that was good enough for me. Of course I would still occasionally look at other attractive women, and men too – that's only natural, as sexuality is a flexible and mysterious thing. But I knew for sure that it had taken a woman to make me feel like a woman, and only by finding Claire had I found myself.

Isn't it funny how life creeps up on you when you're least expecting it?

I WISH

Once upon a rhyme I was just a plain Jane, living in a town where nothing ever happened, protected by my plainness, when I was stopped by one of those market research guys who you would normally pretend not to notice. How ordinary was that?

Except I didn't ignore him, although God only knows why I chose to even give him the time of day. Maybe there was something a little bit other-worldly about him. I was a self-conscious eighteen-year-old girl who preferred to avoid strangers if at all possible, especially if they just happened to be men who were the slightest bit eligible. I would rather die than talk to one of those!

And this man rated eleven out ten on the scale of eligibility. He was handsome to behold – tall, lightly muscular, piercing blue eyes, and what can only be described as presence. Normally, I would have run a mile, back home to where I still lived with my beloved mom and dad, to watch an old episode of *Star Trek*, but I chose to tarry a while. (You'll have to excuse me – I was born into the wrong era. That's why I sometimes talk like a nineteenth-century spinster.)

'Could I borrow some of your precious time and ask you to participate in our survey?' he asked. Naturally, I approved of his style of speech.

'If you so desire,' I hesitantly agreed, sensing my skin beginning to redden. I was hating the fact that my body refused to keep a secret and had to let him know how I really felt.

'That's most kind. It shouldn't take more than a few minutes,' he replied.

'OK, question number one – how often do you attend church?'

'Honestly?'

He nodded.

'Only at Christmas, and family events like weddings and baptisms, I guess.'

'I see,' he said, scribbling on his form.

'So you're not trying to convert me?' I asked, strangely reassured that he represented religion rather than big business.

'Oh heavens no. You need to find your own way.'

'And you're not asking for money?'

'Oh *purlees*! Who or what do you think I am? I am in the employment of God.'

'Oh,' I said pausing to try and make sense of what he'd just said. 'He's a good employer then?' I asked, not at all intending to mock him.

'Hell yes, one of the best – although he can be a bit, how shall we say, capricious.'

'Really?' I said, not quite knowing the full meaning of the word, which I think he must have guessed.

'Liable to change his mind when you least expect it. This survey, for instance – if you can call it that – all stems from that unfortunate business in the Garden of Eden.'

'You don't say,' I said. I sensed that I'd somehow managed to get myself mixed up with an extremely weird person, even if he did happen to look like an angel.

'Look – instead of chatting away in a shopping mall,' he said, spitting out the phrase with distaste, 'why don't we slip into somewhere more comfortable?'

That's when I heard those alarm bells start ringing in my head. So this is what happens when you speak to strange men in the street. I should have listened to what my mother had told me, and been my usual sensible self instead.

'I'm not trying to pick you up, if that's what you're thinking,' he added. 'You're not really my type.'

OK, I have to admit to experiencing a small tinge of regret, but it was mixed with a much larger splash of relief.

'We've already had enough trouble with angels falling in love with their watches and vice-versa' he said. 'Not that I don't think you're lovely,' he quickly added. 'Although you do need to get rid of those glasses, and that brown dress really doesn't do you any favours. No, I'm gay, although we're not supposed to find any mortal attractive – it's against the rules, and it's already led to all sorts of bother – but wait till you see that David Beckham when he grows up. I'm so worried I won't be able to resist him.'

I tried to disguise my shocked expression.

'Sorry, I forgot. You're not quite ready for gay banter yet, are you? After all, it's hardly past 1981. But you will be soon.'

So he wasn't trying to seduce me. Why is it that plain girls always think every man is out to get them? If only!

Perhaps I was intrigued and wanted to know more, even though he was probably certifiably insane.

'I could spare half an hour. There's a diner around the corner,' I said.

'You'll give me that long? That's so brilliant of you, especially when you consider what little time you have left.'

'I beg your pardon. You're talking like I'm about to die?'

'Well yes, of course, eventually, but not for a good while yet, unless you happen to get run over by truck. So much of life is just random.'

We walked into the diner, as unlikely a couple as you've ever seen, a geeky adolescent schoolgirl accompanied by this dashing cool dude. What could the heartthrob possibly see in the geek, I imagined them all thinking. You wouldn't exactly call me confident about myself back in the day, but things were about to change.

'So,' he said after we'd ordered our pancakes and crispy bacon. 'Are you glad that there are currently five churches in your town, spreading the word of the Lord? Although we would only actually recommend three of them,' he said as an afterthought.

'Yes, I am,' I replied. 'It shows that there's more to life in Valley Stream than who can afford the fastest car, the biggest house or the coolest jacket.'

'That's the right answer,' he replied, before taking a mouthful of pancake by way of celebration.

'I didn't know there was such a thing as right and wrong answers when filling in a questionnaire.'

'There is in our line of work,' he replied. 'Anyway, let's forget the survey for now, seeing as you have successfully passed the test.' The waitress poured us two cups of strong Americano coffee. 'Let's get down to business,' he said, his eyes twinkling. He was obviously enjoying this particular part of his duties. 'I am hereby authorised to offer you three wishes as compensation for the rather onerous punishments handed out by God to Eve when she persuaded Adam to eat the apple.'

'Three wishes? I thought that was more to do with fairy tales than religion.'

'God is to do with everything,' he replied.

'Is that so?' was all I could manage to utter.

'It is so,' he said, challenging my apparent disbelief – although the weird thing was, I did believe him. There was something about him, an aura if you will, that gave me the impression he was speaking from the heart.

'But why me?'

'You're a woman, for a start, although you would never have guessed it, as you are a touch dowdy darling – and women are allowed to be glamorous.'

I bridled a little at his criticism. Typical gay angel, wanting all women to dress like Barbie dolls.

'So, here's the thing. We've been sent out by you-know-who to choose a randomly-selected group of women every fall, to kind of soften the blow of what happened to Eve, and its consequent effect on women – having to endure the pain of childbirth, putting up with premenstrual syndrome, not to mention the unsanitary habits of men.'

'That's only fair,' I said. I had always believed that women get a raw deal, so if God wanted to redress the balance a little, then who was I to dismiss it? It's amazing what you can believe when you want something so bad it hurts.

So what did I want to change about myself, or at least needed to improve on? (I assumed it was all about me.) I was happy enough with my mind; God had been generous enough in that respect. I could take on any mental challenge and usually come out on top. In short, I was a brainiac. But looks wise, in my opinion mine left a lot to be desired. It wasn't that I was ugly – more nondescript, like the town I lived in. And why did brainy girls have to be plain? Why couldn't they be beautiful and intelligent at the same time? Suddenly, I wanted it all.

'First wish please,' he said. 'I haven't got all day.'

'OK,' I said, having now totally bought into his project.

'I want to be pretty.'

He paused for a moment while recording my request on an electronic tablet, something I would later recognise as an iPad.

'Good choice,' he said. 'You're so much classier than most girls these days. It's either I want to have bigger boobs or to boost my booty – so obvious – whereas by saying you want to be pretty, you can have the works, and that includes boobs and booty in the package regardless, along with come-to-bed eyes, luscious lips, lustrous long hair, high cheekbones – do you want me to go on?'

Well I did, but I was too shy to admit it.

'And when does all this happen?' I enquired, not quite certain how this new look would be achieved.

'When you go to bed this evening, just dream of how you would like to be, and when you wake up in the morning you can say hello to the new you.'

'That's unbelievable,' I replied.

'And what is more, nobody close to you will notice any difference. They will only have memories of you as the pretty new you, whereas strangers will see this astonishingly beautiful young girl, and so your life can begin.'

'How can I possibly thank you?'

'Simply by believing, and then it will happen. None of this ridiculous nonsense of having to kiss frogs, or being forced to get intimate with tramps, like some of my straight angel colleagues insist on putting you mortals through.'

I was relieved to have jumped the first hurdle, except that now I had to think seriously about what would come next. After all, I'd been granted three wishes, if I'd understood him correctly. A strategy for wishes number two and three slowly began to evolve in my mind. I told you I was brainy.

'Your second wish please,' he said, inspecting his perfectly-manicured nails.

'Yes, I wanted to talk to you about that.'

'Fire away,' he replied.

'Well the first one was easy. I suspect that most girls want to look the best they possibly can – even the brainy ones. But it's such a big responsibility to sit here and think of two more wishes that could irrevocably shape the rest of my life, especially when I don't know what's in store.'

'If you're asking me to predict the future, then that's beyond my powers,' said the gay angel.

'So how about you come back in ten years' time and ask me again, and then I might know what it is I actually need to wish for.'

'Heaven above, that is most unusual, and highly irregular,' he said, slurping another shot of coffee. 'But clever – yes, real clever. And I rather like it.' He stroked his chin, presumably reflecting on what he might or might not be able to grant. 'Oh to hell with it,' he said jumping up from his chair. 'You've already outfoxed me once with your wish to be pretty. Considering it includes that many add-on features, so why shouldn't you be granted a ten-year delay as well?'

'And then if I could be so bold, at our next meeting to be allowed to wait for another decade for wish number three?'

'A wish every ten years? Now you're really pushing it, but I guess it kind of makes sense. Plus, Eve did get a really bum rap, and all of her descendants too, of which of course, you are one.'

'Let's hear it for Eve,' I said. I got up and shook him by the hand.

'It's a deal,' he said, 'and I'll meet you here ten years from now to the time and day, but if you stand me up then the deal is off, and you will forfeit your last two wishes, while your first wish will become null and void. Do you understand?'

'Perfectly,' I replied.

'It's been a pleasure doing business with you – such an intelligent young woman, and a pretty one too, at least by the time you awake in the morning. Sweet dreams.'

We went our separate ways, and strange as it may sound, none of what happened really crossed my mind for the rest of the day, as I was too intent on revising for my entrance examination for Harvard. Not even the promise of becoming pretty was going to knock me off course when it came to pursuing my education. However, I did find just enough time to indulge in a little clothes and make-up shopping. I was going to need a whole new wardrobe for my transformation – such was my belief that this thing really was going to happen.

I received a few mystified looks from confused shop assistants who wondered why I was out buying dresses, tops and skirts that were two sizes too small for me. In the end, I had to invent an imaginary friend – and there was absolutely nothing in brown for the gay angel to get precious about.

I really wasn't sure that I was going to enjoy this whole business of becoming a girlie girl – I certainly didn't want it to take over my life as I'd seen happen with some female friends of mine, who had become utterly obsessed with how they looked to the exclusion of almost everything else. I was happy to return to my studies and get my career as a civil rights lawyer back on track.

It was with a sinking heart that I eventually went to bed. Either I'd been duped by an insane individual who'd been playing on my greatest fears and insecurities or I had opted for a way of life that could wreck the seriousness of my intent as a top lawyer. *Que sera sera*, as that great American philosopher Doris Day would sing on our old record player at home.

And so, for the deepest sleep of my life. I dropped further into unconsciousness than even anaesthetics could deliver, until I was only a few rasping breaths away from death's dark door. So, you can understand why I felt relieved to be still alive when I woke up some eight hours later, feeling a little bleary-eyed.

But what eyes! They were bigger, bolder and smokier than I had ever seen on a girl outside a Hollywood movie. The angel's promise had come true after all.

I won't tell you in too much detail about the other enhancements, for fear of being accused of being mightily vain – except to say that with my little turned-up nose, my astonishingly high cheekbones, my luscious ruby-red lips and that soft-as-morning-dew skin, I was about as pretty as any girl has the right to be. Plus, I'd been given all the other stuff promised as a kind of a bonus, like the prominent 36D boobs and the booty that would have made a Kardashian envious. Why did the angel have to do that? Just straightforward pretty would have been fine by me. I dreaded to think where these angels were getting their inspiration from.

As promised, my mum and dad didn't express any surprise on seeing me at breakfast, apart from commenting that I was looking a bit tired, and claiming that all this schoolwork was doing my health no good at all.

And when I was caught looking at my reflection in a mirror at school, Mrs Monet, the art teacher, commented, 'Yes, you're gorgeous Jane. High time you got used to it.' I wondered if I'd just been on the receiving end of jealousy.

OK, I have to admit to being shocked by being asked out by at least three different boys in my first day as the new me, while all the modish girls simply ached to be my friend. Yet it didn't impress me at all as I had only one thing on mind, Harvard, and studying under the almightily charismatic lecturer there, Professor Luther Jeremiah Humble, who had the same effect on me as film stars and former members of the Backstreet Boys had on more typical girls.

I'd read all about him in the top legal journals. He was nearly twenty years older, but still I reckoned he had what it took to become my ideal partner, because here was a man who would be on the same intellectual level as me. Not that I had an unduly big opinion of myself – I'm only stating a fact of life. And thanks to the gay angel, I now had the means to make him aware of my presence.

So through sheer hard work I achieved the required grades to gain admission to my preferred course at the university of my dreams. My mom and dad were thrilled for me, although there were others who argued, why on earth did I want to be bothering with education when I had the looks that would guarantee me a rich husband at the drop of a false eyelash? My parents were so much more advanced than that in their thinking, while I have to admit that my prettiness soon became irksome to me, as I wanted to be judged primarily for my intellect, not for the way I looked.

There was something deeply annoying about how people now spoke to me, either with too much awe or reverence, which was usually the case with geeky boys, or like I was a little bit simple, as if someone with that much beauty couldn't possibly be lucky enough to be intelligent as well.

This continued right up to and beyond my first day at Harvard Law School, with some admittedly handsome young men offering to carry my briefcase, or opening doors for me in corridors, no doubt hoping for other kinds of favours from me in return. But I had eyes only for the man who'd just walked into our lecture hall to instruct us all in the field of human rights: our lecturer and professor, and the man of my dreams, who I was telling you about earlier.

To say he had a reputation was putting it mildly, not only as a great legal advocate but also as a ladies' man who had become infamous for his countless affairs, more often than not with students in his care. Highly unprofessional, of course, and I intended to rectify his ways, but not until after he'd met me.

This is where my mystic makeover would finally come into its own. I would use my beauty to grab his attention and then my brains to impress him, dressing as perkily as Ivy League convention would allow while showering him with insightful questions and ground-breaking answers at every opportunity. So what if I inspired one or two thinly-veiled looks of hatred from a few of the more stunning girls on the course? I hadn't gone to all this trouble to impress them, had I?

But more importantly, the Prof only seemed to have eyes for me. I reciprocated with the smokiest stare I could manage in return, which drew him back to me with ever-increasing frequency, except when he had to consult some case notes on the 1968 Washington riots.

'Right once again, Miss Pendleton,' he announced as I answered another of his questions on jurisprudence correctly.

'Call me Jane,' I rather forwardly replied.

'I would like you to visit me in my chambers after the lecture, Miss er... I mean, Jane, if you will.'

You could hear the other students' suppressed laughter straining to get out, creating strange noises like breaking wind. How immature of them.

'You appear to have some interesting views on habeas corpus which I think we might want to explore further,' he said, as if to try and justify himself. Even I could see through that one.

When I entered his room he adopted a pose of studied indifference, whereas I suspected, and certainly hoped, that he was in truth yearning for me sorely. Forgive me if I appear immodest, but it's really not me I'm talking about, more this other glamorous girl I had become. And as far as I was concerned, it was simply a means to an end, a way of getting noticed so he could fall in love with me, and let's face it, the look of a woman is where most men prefer to start.

He reacted dismissively, as if he'd already forgotten about our appointment, when it was so obviously the first thing on his mind.

'Thank you for taking the time to see me,' I said politely, my words not really matching my new sexy image. I should have been pouting and purring like Olivia Newton John after her makeover in *Grease*, proclaiming, tell me about it stud!

'So you believe in the concept of human rights. What is your opinion of governments who attempt to redefine it?' he asked me.

'Mostly I'm against. It's usually an excuse for right wing regimes to find ways around acknowledging their responsibilities to protect their citizens from gross abuse by corrupt legal systems…'

I went on and on. I could sense he was listening to me quite intently at first, and then you could see his mind beginning to wander. How I hoped I wasn't boring him.

'Would you like to continue our discussion over a meal at a delightful Italian restaurant I know?' was his only response to my comprehensive answer to his question about human rights.

I guess I should have been thrilled. I guess that line had worked for him a hundred times before, which probably accounted for why he looked so perplexed upon hearing my reply.

'I'm not really that hungry,' I said.

'I was only trying to be friendly,' he said, sounding a touch hurt.

'Can I speak to you without fear or favour?'

'Go ahead,' he said, but like he didn't mean it.

'Please don't imagine that I'm not longing to jump into bed with you and feel your body next to mine, but I really don't want to finish up as just another notch on your bedpost.'

'I resent your implication,' he snorted, huffing and puffing like a maiden aunt whose honour had been offended.

'You see, I want to be the one.' He gave me a most curious stare, but I continued regardless. 'So, you find me attractive – and that's great – all part of my ultimate plan – but it means I've only got as far as first base. So if I give in now to your magnetic attraction, I will lose you forever. I'll become just another of a long line of girls who you have lured into your bed only to be kicked out in the morning, never to be invited again.'

'Are you some kind of stalker?'

'Don't be so defensive,' I chided him. 'I'm the woman who has what it takes to change your life for the better. I want to you to feel about me the way I feel about you, and should that ever happen, then we can start talking about making love, whereas if we did it now – and don't think I'm not sorely tempted – it would only be about having sex.'

'Well thank you for opening up your feelings to me,' he said holding his hand out, 'but from now on I think our relationship should remain purely academic.'

'Don't be afraid to fall in love – and if it should be with me, that would be miraculous,' I said, returning his handshake. It was only later that I learnt that it was at that moment when he lost his heart to me. However, it took him a whole semester to face up to his feelings and finally give love a chance. There were already signs along the way. Within days of our first encounter he stopped dating students, much to the distress of the pretty girls who already despised me in our class.

'What have you done to him?' one of them cried out loud at a drunken student party one Saturday evening.

'Nothing that he doesn't want to do himself,' I replied, creating more confusion than clarity in her mind, I suspect.

And more than once in class I noticed him becoming unexpectedly tongue-tied whenever he glanced in my direction, until one extraordinary day he came to a complete standstill while addressing the issue of innocent until proven guilty.

The class looked on in astonishment. It was like he was falling apart in front of us.

'And if it is assumed that guilt, or indeed innocence, cannot be, er… verified,' he began, before quickly stalling again.

We all looked on in shock and embarrassment. How were the mighty fallen!

'Oh for fuck's sake, Jane, will you marry me?'

I wasn't expecting that. And I could have done without the swearing. All I wanted was to be his one and only girlfriend. Marriage had never really crossed my mind at that stage – it was far too much to hope for. Hence the agonising delay in my reply.

'Say something, anything,' one of the pretty girl students pleaded on behalf of everybody in the room. It must have been excruciating for them to witness.

'I do,' I replied. Well, what did you expect me to say?

They all broke out cheering, and shouting and clapping, while I joined him at the front of the class for our first kiss. How extraordinary was that, only getting as far as kissing after he'd proposed marriage, like something out of the nineteenth century, which after all was where I truly belonged.

Also, I'm pleased to report that the kiss was lovely, and tender, and as sexy as hell. I could have torn his clothes off there and then. I reckon some of the students might have enjoyed that kind of thing. But we didn't have to wait long before we consummated our union – I wasn't so nineteenth century that I was delaying until we were married.

In fact, I doubt there had ever been a more enthusiastic virgin than me. I had previously needed to exercise so much self-control in order to lure him to the party that I wasn't going to let a little thing like losing my virginity get in the way. Not that he wasn't slightly astonished when I told him about how I was still *virgo intacta*. He appeared visibly moved at the thought of it, even stopping him in his tracks during the early stages of our love making – that was until I moved my hand towards the front of his pants, where I had been aching for it to travel for so long.

I adored it just that little bit more than I was frightened by it, while touching him intimately seemed to have the desired effect of getting him back in the bedroom.

'I promise to be gentle,' he reassured me. 'I would never want to hurt you.'

He began to take control, gently peeling off my silk blouse and balconette bra, licking, tantalising and arousing those darling buds of May.

I closed my eyes as he began to awake me from my sexual slumber by first using his touch, appearing to know me more intimately than I knew myself.

He spent forever first relaxing then exciting me, heightening my senses until I began dreading yet longing for the moment we would become one.

'Are you OK?' He asked with kindness, care and concern etched on his lovely black face. I knew he was holding back, thinking only of my needs, until he at long last entered me as gently as a man of his magnitude was able.

I almost forgot to breathe, before letting out a little yelp of pain, or was it pleasure?

And then after a few tentative moves inside me the Prof paused for further guidance.

'I'm not hurting you?'

'Only as much as I want to be,' I shamelessly replied, his cue to move a little quicker.

Oh, how I now loved feeling every adorable inch of him inside me.

'Harder,' I begged of him. 'I want to be well and truly fucked by you.'

I couldn't believe I'd just said that. Sex can make you say the most awful things.

And by the time we made love for the third time in just under two hours I experienced my first orgasm – or at least that's what I thought it was – like a bomb packed full of pleasure had just exploded deep inside of me and was now reverberating around my body where everything tingled with such intensity that I wanted to scream out, this is fucking Jim, but not as we know it.

Nothing could have prepared me for anything this unbelievably climactic.

'So this is what I've been missing,' I said as we completed our best ever session of love making so far.

'Is it always this good?' I asked him.

'With me? Yes, and I hope it will get even better,' he not so modestly replied.

But the Prof was as good as his word – I suspect he was something of a master in the art of lovemaking – and while I had nothing to compare it with I just knew I would never need to look elsewhere to find proof that he was as good as it gets, however curious I might one day become.

There was only one guy I would ever want, and that was the Prof. And as far as I knew, that was also the way he felt about me, which in a sense was a touch more amazing, as he'd been on a journey from serial cheat to monogamous husband, and then expectant father.

I gave thanks to the power of love.

In time we were blessed with three beautiful children, two girls and a boy. I hate to write that ours was the perfect marriage, as in a sense, there is no such thing, but it was as near darn perfect as a union of man and woman could be – this side of heaven.

We also went into legal partnership with one another, representing oppressed minorities in court cases while continuing to lecture at Harvard to supplement our income, and further our academic careers.

So after nine and three quarter years I began to wonder what it was that I could possibly wish for when the gay Angel next came to visit. After all, I'd gone from the girl who wanted it all to the woman who had everything.

I couldn't miss my appointment with my ethereal mentor at the Diner in Valley Stream though, as I knew there would be dire consequences if I did. I had to invent a whole bunch of excuses both to my kids and my husband to explain my absence. I hated lying to them – it was possibly the first time I had ever deceived the Prof – but what else could I say? – that I'd got an appointment with an Angel who was about to grant me my second wish. Sorry, but that would always have to remain a secret in our house.

I hung around outside the appointed diner in downtown Valley Stream trying to look inconspicuous. I'd never been stood up by an angel before, but there was no sign of him wherever I looked. And then he materialised as if from nowhere, looking fabulously weighed down by bling, made even more conspicuous by his painted pink nails and an extravagant fedora hat.

'I see you're keeping a low profile,' I said teasing him.

'Well you might have forgotten what I look like. It's been ten years since we last met, and for you that's an eternity.'

He was right. He almost always was.

'So how have you been keeping?'

'Nothing I say can really properly answer that question. I'm a different person now, not only in the way I look, but my priorities are all changed now.'

'That's what is called growing up. It's just that you've

been subjected to a more extreme version of it than most.'

I ordered a skinny latte coffee while he got a cappuccino, plus some really strange looks.

'And how has the new look been working for you?' he asked me.

'It achieved what it set out to do, and that was to catch the attention of the Prof.'

'So you'd like to be plain Jane again.'

'Not at all, but neither am I obsessed with it, and I really only want to look good for my man.'

'What a waste,' he replied.

'OK, so I don't exactly object to the occasional admiring glance, but that's about as flighty as I'm going to get.'

'I never doubted it,' he replied.

'The whole focus of my life has changed since having children. Now I see everything in relation to them, keeping them safe, making them happy, planning for their future. Nothing else seems to matter anymore, and I love it.'

He patted me on my forearm I supposed to confirm his approval, or was he being condescending towards me? You could never quite tell.

'So, it's make your mind up time. What's your next wish going to be?' he asked.

'I can't see beyond my children,' I said. 'The Prof and I have everything we want. We couldn't be happier. It's my kids I worry about, every hour and every minute of the day. There are so many dangers out there. I want you to keep them safe.'

'Wish granted,' he replied. 'So see you in ten years then, same time, same place.' He gathered his stuff in preparation for his exit. 'Must dash – I've got front row tickets for this new all-male dance troop, the Chippendales. I believe they nearly get naked.'

'That's outrageous. No respectable woman would ever pay to go and see that.'

I obviously still had some growing up to do.

And so our life as a family continued to be about as idyllic as the Waltons, while our legal practise became internationally renowned. We were representing the downtrodden and the oppressed against some of the most powerful in the land, and we almost always won. But our children continued to be the ultimate focus of our lives. I watched them grow towards adulthood in what seemed like minutes rather than years, their childhoods disappearing in the slipperiness of time. But I was always consoled by knowing they were in good hands, watched over by an angel who (when he wasn't doing his nails) would be keeping them safe from harm, which made me the most relaxed mother around.

What I hadn't accounted for was – who was overlooking the Prof, the man I worshipped and adored, while the risks of the world besieged us? When I first heard that knock I didn't really sense anything untoward – until I saw the two big burly policemen standing outside my door.

'Mrs Humble?' said one of them.

'Yes?'

'I am sorry, but we have some bad news for you. Maybe you should sit down.'

I didn't need to hear any more. I knew I'd lost him. I always used to admonish the Prof for driving too fast, while he would joke in return that it was only because he wanted to get back to me as soon as possible. But this time, it would be never again.

Almost everything the policeman said went right over my head yet, except for the occasional word. A pile-up on the highway – killed instantly – he wouldn't have suffered.

'The angel should have been looking after him,' was all I could say. I'm sure the two policemen had heard weirder stuff than that when having to deliver such dreadful news.

I could have gone numb, or more likely fallen apart, but I had to stay strong for my children, if you could call them that any more, as they were now 19, 18 and 16 respectively.

We were all devastated in our respective ways, but we worked our way through our grief. My two older kids eventually went back to their respective universities to continue their studies, while Sophie and I tried our hardest to live normal, happy fulfilled lives. Unfortunately, it never felt much more than an act.

How could we possibly fill such a gaping void in our lives? But life had to go on, if not for me, then for my children, and soon Sophie left home to study too, leaving me alone, awaiting the next visitation of the angel, which was still a year away. I had so many questions to ask, and so much anger to deal with. In the meantime I returned to lecturing at Harvard, where students watched me in awed silence, no doubt wondering how the hell I was able to function after what I'd been through.

It was the nights that were worst, for I never missed him more than when I was alone in our bed. The guilt tortured me even more intensely when I began to find one or two of my students attractive, even going as far as fantasising about making love to one of them. It was as if I was being unfaithful to the Prof, whereas in reality it was proof that I was entering recovery, although I still had a long way to go.

You see before the Prof, sex had never played much of a role in my life, but during our time it was the glue that held us together. Now I longed for it again, yet just the thought of wanting it, while thrilling, also made me sick with remorse. And would anybody find me attractive anymore? These days I only received looks of pity, not desire or passion – was I going to have to get used to that?

I know it's wrong for lecturers to go lusting after students, but if the Prof hadn't desired me, we would never have had three beautiful children and the nineteen happiest years of my life. And as long as I didn't act on my desires, where was the harm in it? And how could you not be in lust with some of the young men who studied in my course?

But it was all academic when it came down to it, because nobody, either male or female, seemed to notice me. They just saw the faded, middle-aged lecturer at the front of the class, the careworn shopper standing in line at the supermarket or the sad widow at the social function. I was that anonymous woman you half-see everywhere you go.

At least the gay angel seemed pleased to see me when we met once more at the Valley Stream Diner. I guess we had developed something of a bond over the years.

'They're all using this place now,' he said, pointing towards a dishevelled hobo talking to a careworn middle-aged woman. 'I know him. He's one of us, but his dining companion doesn't yet know it. What's he playing at?'

'I'm glad I've got you as my angel.'

'I guess you don't want me to ask how your ten years has been?'

'Most of it was wonderful, until…'

'I know,' he said patting me on the hand. 'There was nothing we could do to stop it, you know. Life can be so random, and it most certainly wasn't planned.'

'I know that should make me feel better. It's just that I feel so guilty, having asked you to look out for my kids, yet I totally neglected the Prof. It feels like I'm to blame for his death.'

'It was his reckless driving that killed him, nothing else, and he accepts that.'

'You've spoken to him – since his death?' I enquired in astonishment.

'We had a frothy together.'

'A frothy?'

'It's our version of coffee, except it's heavenly, and tastes even better than it smells.'

'And he's OK?'

'He's fine.'

'And is he missing me as much as I am missing him?'

'More so.'

'Has he got a message for me?'

'He says he's so utterly sorry for being that careless with his life, and jeopardising what mattered to him above all – you. And now that your children have grown up he wants you to enjoy yourself, just as he used to.'

It was as if the Prof could read my mind. I didn't need to ask whether I would see him again, so I supposed I might as well begin to live a little while I awaited our inevitable reunion. And what's more, I had the Prof's consent.

'I don't want to rush you,' said the Gay Angel, 'but are you ready to make your third and final wish?'

'I think so,' I replied, 'assuming that getting the Prof back isn't an option.'

'I'm afraid not. Death is a bummer.'

'OK.'

'Go ahead.'

'I want to be noticed.'

He wrote it down. 'Would you like to elaborate?'

'You probably wouldn't understand. It's a thing that happens mostly to middle-aged women – we become invisible to others, like ghosts, people who have died before their time.'

'How ghastly,' he observed. 'I would hate not to be noticed.' That was never going to happen to him.

'How times change,' he observed. 'Twenty years ago you couldn't bear to attract attention. But isn't it just a little bit similar to your first wish, wanting to be transformed? I'm not sure I can allow that.'

'I'm not looking for another radical makeover. That's the last thing I want. This time I want you to enhance my spirit, so that I am worth knowing again.'

'Far more important! Wish granted – consider it done,' he said, rising from his seat to prepare for his next consultation.

'Before I go, you've got to watch this,' he said, gesturing towards a forlorn middle-aged woman who sat opposite the hobo, as she leant over to kiss him forcibly on the lips.

'Oh gross!' said an elderly woman with purple hair.

'I'm leaving, and I suggest you do, too. Too many angels for one diner,' he said, escorting me on to the street. And in a second he was gone. All that was left was a puff of smoke.

'I can't stand long goodbyes,' I heard him say, his voice trailing into the distance.

'Just as well,' I replied, doubting whether he'd heard me.

As for my final wish, I struggled to get used to it, for just as promised, whenever I walked into a room, a bus, or a train, heads would inevitably turn in my direction. Exactly quite why, I wasn't too sure, but having grieved for long enough, I can't deny that it did me a power of good. Not that I had any intention of doing anything with this new-found power of mine, for my heart still belonged firmly to the Prof, and to look at anybody else still felt like I was betraying him.

So when a young African-American student started staring dreamily at me with loving eyes, I initially remained unmoved by the whole business. After all, it's quite normal for students to develop crushes on lecturers, as I, above all people, know. And regardless of the fact that I'd found the love of my life as a student while longing for my lecturer, it was hardly appropriate behaviour, especially as this young man was in my care.

Yet why was it so much more shocking that a young male student should desire an older female tutor? Double standards, that's what I called it. It almost became a legal principle with me, wanting to prove the case, that older women have a right to be attracted to younger men, and vice versa.

Well OK, I guess it kind of helped that he was such a likeable young guy. His name was Aaron Wise, and he was big in the college football team. He was a man mountain of a young guy, blessed with a radiant smile which complemented his soulful deep brown eyes.

So what if I might have been a little bit smitten? I started to invent reasons why he should visit my office, and thankfully he showed no reticence in accepting my varied invitations. Then he started turning up outside unannounced with some lame excuse about not understanding *amicus curae* – as if!

'Why don't we discuss this over a meal at my place?' I suggested to Aaron. 'And let's keep this between ourselves, shall we? You know how the class will talk.' He wasted no time in accepting my invitation. Suffice to say, we never got round to eating that meal – dear reader, I had him. We went straight to bed instead, desperate to devour one another for our respective reasons. And he was right for me – firm, taut, muscular, tender, passionate, long-lasting and generously male – not only a great lover, but a fine talker too. He reminded me how I once used to feel about wanting to represent the oppressed and underprivileged.

How could I not warm to him? Yet I feared he would view our love-making as a one-off experience, something to tell his football buddies about in the shower before he moved on to younger, prettier women. But I was wrong. He wanted to see me again and again at my home, where we became ever closer, talking and loving and walking and cooking and showering together. I would soap his divine manhood before blowing away the foam – sorry, too much information – before debating which was best, Star Wars or Star Trek. Yes, it was that serious.

I guess I ought to have spoken to the university authorities about what was going on between us. It could affect Aaron's grades, and therefore his ultimate career and his precious future. Or maybe it would just fizzle out, a student's short-lived obsession with his teacher, or a sad, lonely lecturer coming to her senses after being forced to let a young student go. I was over twenty years his senior, after all, and he would be wanting children while I would be longing for relaxing weekends in Florida playing Scrabble with senior citizens in loud shirts. It was never going to work.

When one of my female students – a girl I'd nicknamed Betty Boop, for her large eyes and extravagant eye lashes – started making sarcastic remarks about the time I was spending on Aaron, I began to panic about where this was leading.

'I guess a tutorial would be too much to ask for?' she asked, and upon seeing me hesitate, continued, 'Oh how silly of me, I expect Aaron has got them all booked up.'

Ouch! Young girls can be so cruel.

So when he started talking about taking our relationship to the next level I knew I had to end it there and then, however much I thought about how close we'd become with our shared obsessions about life, liberty and Klingons.

'You need to let me go, Aaron, and find somebody your own age,' I counseled him.

'Why would I want to do that? Young women bore me,' he replied.

'Everything might seem OK now, but just wait until I hit fifty and you're still in your twenties. What are you going to think then?'

'Age is just a number,' he replied. 'It means precisely zero.'

'We really ought to end it now,' I pleaded with him.

'Will you marry me?' he said in desperation, getting down on one knee.

'No, I damn well won't!'

'So what else can I do to make you want me?'

'Nothing at all. It was fun while it lasted, but it's over now.'

Maybe I was practicing tough love. I'm sure the Prof must have said exactly the same thing to many of his student lovers. I had become no better than him in his bad old days, if not worse.

With that Aaron walked out the door and left me, and I lost the best thing I'd ever had.

Yet if I could sleep with one young man, why not enjoy a few more? So it was that I took consolation in one hot student after another. I was behaving like a wanton woman who had totally lost control. There was something about the sweet smell of them, the high octane power, and their vulnerability too. While they had the energy, I had the know-how – a perfect combination. That's why mature women and young men go so well together. It's nature's naughty little secret!

I'm not sure the Prof would have approved though – not on account of my salacious behaviour alone but because he wanted me to be happy. And apart from that adorable adrenalin rush of excitement, I was far from being a contented lady once those divine love-making sessions had finished. In truth, I'd never felt more alone.

Plus, unsurprisingly, I started to get a reputation. That led to me being called in by the Chancellor who warned me about consorting with students. I was really mad.

'Well, you never told the Prof that when he was playing around,' I said as I stormed out of his office. 'A perk of the job for a man, I guess, but when it's a woman doing the same thing you start threatening her with losing her job. Call that justice? It's an absolute disgrace!'

That outburst made me feel better just for a short while, but even with a different young man in my bed almost every night, I had become the loneliest woman in New England. Where was the Gay Angel when I needed him? But I had run out of wishes anyway.

And then, one day while I was delivering a lecture on adversary proceeding, it struck me how totally dumb I had been. The real love of this second period of my life had been under my nose all along.

'A lawsuit which arises in a bankruptcy case begins by filing a…' I began, and then, unaccountably, I came to a grinding halt. The students were as bored as I was, but my breakdown roused them from their stupor.

'Sorry,' I said.

You see, at long last it had finally dawned upon me that Aaron must be the one, because if he was willing to deal with the age difference, then why shouldn't I? Especially as I was the net beneficiary of the proposed arrangement, whereas he had more to lose. And why shouldn't he have the right to make his own choice about the consequences of our age difference? Why should I make decisions on his behalf about what was best for him? I was still worth having, wasn't I? And surely I could still make him happy?

I now knew so much more about men, but it was probably all too late anyway. Best try to get on with the lecture.

'So when a trial takes place within the context of a bankruptcy case... oh fuck it! Aaron, have you got a serious girlfriend yet?'

'No miss.'

'Me neither.'

I heard Betty Boop snigger at me. I remembered when my beloved Prof had proposed to me in class. Now I longed for Aaron to do the same. Deep down, I was still an old-fashioned girl at heart.

'I mean I haven't found a boyfriend,' I quickly added.

'I'm so glad to hear it,' Aaron said with a rising sense of joy in his voice. He stood up and approached the front of the class.

'Jane, will you do me the great honour of becoming my wife?'

I don't know why, but I kept him waiting a few agonising seconds. Maybe I didn't want to appear too willing, given my recent reputation.

'I completely and irrevocably do,' I eventually replied.

We hugged and kissed as the classroom cheered, even Betty Boop. I was dismissed from my job for conduct unbecoming, but what did I care? I had Aaron, didn't I?

And I never regretted it. It was as if my life was starting all over again, except this time I didn't need an angel on hand to make it happen. We lived pretty much happily ever after, or at least as much as anyone can outside a fairy tale.

When my dismissal from Harvard as a senior lecturer was upheld, what did I go and do? I became an instructor in ballroom dancing of course. I had always been a fan of *Dancing With The Stars* – who wasn't in those days? – so I started my own dance studio. After a tricky first few months as I set about learning everything from the waltz to the Argentinian tango, it went from strength to strength.

Aaron meanwhile pursued his legal studies unhindered by my presence at Harvard, but I was there for him when he came home at night, where it was always heavenly whatever we finished up doing together – and yes, it was usually that. We once role-played Spock and Lieutenant Uhura in our bedroom, uniforms and all, in honour of our shared devotion to the classic television and film series.

And did I ever meet the Gay Angel again? Only when I died, but I don't much like talking about that – except to say that it was wonderful to reconnect with the Prof again, although I missed Aaron so much it hurt, and I later learnt that he was heartbroken too.

'Tell him to go live again and find somebody else,' I pleaded with the Gay Angel, and he agreed to deliver my message back to Aaron on earth. But I was a little taken aback when Aaron decided to hook up with, and then eventually marry, Betty Boop, while I lived happily ever after up above with my beloved Prof.

What in heaven's name was I going to do when Aaron's day finally came and he ascended up into the clouds, to live forever in the hereafter too, and what would happen to the Prof and me as a consequence? Trouble in paradise?

Heaven is a place where you never have to make impossible choices, and even men should be capable of understanding a woman's unfortunate predicament.

But I feared for the worst. It never ends, does it?

WHY ME?

As their sixtieth wedding anniversary approached, Walt was still wondering why Belinda had chosen him, of all men. Back in the day, he hadn't been the smartest or the coolest or the most handsome of her suitors, whereas she was renowned as a great beauty, and had numerous admirers. A gangly, stumbling boy from the eleventh grade, he knew he wasn't the most obvious choice, so he felt he had to do something desperate and outrageous to attract the attention of the most desired girl in Valley Stream.

What could he possibly do to get Belinda to focus her feelings on him? Perhaps he should shin up a drainpipe and enter her bedroom in the middle of the night to deliver her a bouquet of red roses or a box of the finest Swiss chocolates, or maybe a tight-fitting pink sweater –

he hadn't failed to notice that she loved wearing those – but he decided that that would not be dramatic enough to win over her heart.

So that's why he proposed marriage to her on only his second visit to her parents' house. It was an insane thing for a seventeen-year-old boy to do, yet to his astonishment, she accepted.

Now what was he supposed to do? His mom and dad weren't exactly pleased, nor Belinda's folks. In fact they ganged up to try and persuade the pair that they were far too immature to be even considering such a massive step. But nothing would distract them from their plan. Belinda was perhaps even more committed to going ahead with their teenage wedding than the unlikely boy who started it.

'Everybody's bound to think it's a shotgun wedding,' said Walt's mom at one of their war counsels, and nobody disagreed. They were united in opposing it, but when it comes to common sense versus love, there can only be one winner.

Reluctantly both sets of parents eventually consented, sensing that this wasn't some seven-day wonder but a union that was destined to last. How wise were they? Very, as it worked out. They brought their knowledge and wisdom to bear on the young couple to help them in the practicalities of making their dream come true.

But what about the sex thing? They couldn't help him with that, could they? Worryingly, he was still a virgin, which was pretty much typical back in the fifties. He assumed, wrongly as it turned out, that she was too.

On their wedding night, overcome with nerves, he at first failed to express his love for her, but being far more experienced in the physical arts, she was able to put him at his ease. She stroked his forehead and kissed his ears, telling him not to worry and then lulling him into a strange kind of half-sleep. When she guessed that he was totally relaxed, she raised herself up above him and stole his virginity as if in a dream.

They lay silently in the afterglow of their brief moment of passion until Walt began kissing her again, first tentatively, then enthusiastically, until he was in the ascendant, if only for a short while. How she loved him for it, and for much else too.

Through the years Walt tried his darndest to become a thoughtful and considerate lover, though he never managed to move mountains. However she brought him more joy in the bedroom than he had ever realised was either possible or legal.

But above all, they became good companions and the closest of friends, and their friendship became the rock on which their marriage was built.

In spite of wearing his ring with pride, she continued to receive many uninvited overtures from other men, usually more handsome and charismatic, who, besotted by her great beauty, pursued her relentlessly, yet still she did her best to remain faithful to him. It would have been enough to turn almost any woman's head. Every one of their five children was his (in truth, perhaps she'd been lucky, as she had not always managed to resist those suitors of hers) and as time began to run its inevitable course ten grandchildren and five great grandchildren followed, and counting. They had created a whole clan, and on it would go, but still he didn't know why she had chosen him, when all around her better boys than him had stood in line for her favours.

A week before their 60th wedding anniversary, Walt finally plucked up the courage to ask her the question that had been troubling him for four decades.

'Why me, Belinda, when you could have had anybody you wanted?'

She blushed, even after all those years. He liked that about her.

'Oh, get away with you,' she said.

'But you had the boys of Valley Stream at your feet. You could have had any of them. Why me?'

'I thought you knew,' she replied, pouring out two cups of coffee as they relaxed on their porch on a warm spring morning.

'I'm the luckiest man alive, but I have no idea why.'

'It goes like this,' she said, taking a deep breath before continuing. 'The first time you came round to our house – not the time you proposed, the time before that – I so wanted to look good for a young gentleman I was seeing later that evening, and then you came knocking at the door. I wasn't exactly thrilled to see you, and what's more, my curling irons wouldn't work. I invited you in anyway, and when I told you about my predicament – of course I never mentioned the date – you came to my rescue. First you pulled a screwdriver out of your top pocket and changed the plug on my irons. And then I saw the smile on your face at having done something to make me happy. I knew at that moment that not only were you practical, you were kind. So although I went ahead with my date that night, romanced by the handsomest guy in the county and looking glamorous with my curls, I found myself thinking about you.'

'You don't say,' he said. 'And all because I changed a plug.'

'It's what it represented to me,' she explained to him patiently, as he had become a little deaf in the intervening years. 'When you proposed marriage after only your second visit to our home I was a little shocked, but I thought, why waste any more time looking for Mr Right when I had already found what I'd been searching for? And I had this sense you would know how to treat a woman. And you did know, eventually.'

Now it was his turn to blush, and she rather liked him for it. 'We couldn't have talked like this all those years ago,' he observed.

'Very true,' she replied. 'So while we're on the subject, what was it that you liked about me?'

'Ah, that's easy.'

'Typical man.'

'No, it was so much more than that – it was the fact that you needed me, that I'd come to the rescue of a beautiful girl by repairing those darn irons, and that I could be of some use to you.'

'I see,' said Belinda.

'Mind you, if I'd have known it was for the benefit of another guy...'

She coughed a certain kind of cough, which he knew only too well after nearly sixty years of marriage was code for 'change the subject or else' Maybe she had become a little shy at the power she'd once exercised over other men, at least when it affected her husband.

'We've got a lot to thank those blessed curling irons for,' she said having recovered her voice, 'because it was changing that plug which showed me what you were all about. Practical and kind, not to mention thoughtful. But if I could only have one of those features in a husband, it would be kindness, and that was your greatest quality of all. And I was so right about you.'

Then, to her astonishment, Walt went down on one knee.

'Will you marry me?' he asked of her.

'We are married, silly,' she replied.

'Well, would you marry me, if you had your time again?'

'I would,' she said.

And so they renewed their vows, in church, on the day of their diamond anniversary, with their family all around them.

Well – it would have been unkind not to, wouldn't it?

And so we move to later that evening – here's Belinda,

having already drunk two large glasses of dry sherry at their anniversary party, to introduce some of her guests to you, while I, your narrator, go away to paint my nails…

Where to begin? I'll start with my grand-daughter Annie, a bit of a flibbertigibbet if the truth be known, with her sensible barber-shop-singing husband, Brian. So ill-suited on the surface, yet they always appeared so blissfully happy together. A little like Walt and me, in so many ways, which is probably why I could relate to them so much.

Walt won't be hearing this, will he? Just as well he's asleep in his chair.

She reminded me of me in my youth, devoted to my husband yet tempted by those handsome young men who still pursued me, regardless of me not giving them the slightest hint of encouragement. I'm wandering a little off track – it must be the sherry!

Anyway, Brian, who was something of a singer, was threatening to serenade us with a timeless classic. Over my dead body!

Another great-granddaughter and a great beauty, Caroline, had flown all the way from England with her next door neighbour, Larry, who I have to admit was every inch the dashing British gentleman. Don't tell Walt, but had I been twenty years younger… Hush my mouth as Caro would say – she'd been raised in Alabama and had all the presence of a classic Southern Belle. They appeared entranced by one another and who could blame them? And what with them living next door to each other, they must have had a fine time together on their neighborhood watch patrols, most probably in the middle of the night!

Next there was our great-grand daughter, poor Madison – nature favoured the conception of women in our family – who'd been having serious mental health issues following a long spell of treatment in a high profile medical institution – only the best for our family. She was accompanied by another handsome fellow called Aragorn, who strangely, looked different every time I set eyes on him, as if he was becoming more familiar to me by the minute, reminding of me of some of those handsome beaux who'd set their cap at me in days gone by. I found him most distracting – probably the effect of drinking too much sherry. Even at my great age he was making me feel a little hot and bothered.

Please forgive me. So, her medical supervisor and therapist, a lady by the name of Ella, had called earlier in the week to sanction the day release, saying a trip out could be beneficial for her, but not to believe everything Madison said. In spite of Ella's obvious concern, was it really necessary to lock a young girl away like this? I reckon all she needed was one of my famous hugs. I will see what I can do for her later, and maybe she won't have to go back to that institution ever again.

Now come the celebrities in the family – first our daughter Jacqui, one of the most famous lesbians in the land following her shock divorce from her cheating husband, Senator Jeff Keane. You must have read about it, or seen it reported on TV. And now she's remarried, to a woman no less – a lovely lady called Claire, our new daughter-in-law. We were so pleased for them. Just goes to show that some things do improve with time, once we'd managed to get our heads around it, as the young people are inclined to say.

And then – every party should have one truly outrageous family member – our niece, the divine Adrienne, infamous the world over as the managing director of a global male striptease franchise, accompanied by her new husband – how can I put this politely? I can't – he's called Dick. He used to be a stripper himself before his enforced retirement due to an unfortunate posing pouch malfunction. She had threatened that Dick might come out of hibernation just for one night at our anniversary party. Don't even think of it, I reprimanded her, although had it been a ladies' only event, who knows?

In spite of her fruity language when she describes one of her latest dancer's dangly bits, I have to admit to loving the life force that is Adrienne. She knows what a certain kind of woman enjoys, so she it gives to them, with bells on, whereas Walt reckons she's most likely a witch, who secretly communes with evil spirits. No wonder he felt uncomfortable around her.

Then finally let us raise a glass to absent friends – the greatest loss in our life, which almost destroyed us, our beloved daughter Jane, who tragically passed away in her prime after a distinguished career as a civil rights lawyer, a lecturer in law at Harvard University and a ballroom dance tutor. She was as proud of that last one as the first two, which always used to make us smile. No parent should ever have to bury a child, but photos of her were everywhere to be seen in our house. She would never be forgotten in many other homes too, where her memory would be revered for as long as the sun rose every morning. And above all, we had her three darling children to cherish as well.

Those memories of Jane were running through my mind when suddenly I turned around in surprise as a feather floated down from somewhere on high.

'Interesting folk you've got here', said a flamboyantly-dressed gentleman resplendent in a white floppy hat. He was standing majestically in our hallway, examining his pink painted nails. I rather liked him. I'd always had a penchant for effete men since I'd gotten older. Nobody knew who he was, or who'd invited him, until he revealed that he was a friend of Jane's. Walt wasn't sure about him at first, but he would always be welcome in our house, whoever he was.

But enough of him – let's get back to those relatives of ours. They were a mighty strange bunch, mostly of dubious reputation, but they were ours, and that was all that mattered to me. You see, we can't all be angels, can we?

I must go – we've got a wedding cake to cut.

'Walt – wake up!' – I shouted a little too desperately into his good ear. My heart raced in dread at his complete lack of response. All color had drained from his face, leaving him looking deathly white. Not on this day, of all days, I wanted to scream as I squeezed his freezing hand.

I was surely too late – he must have passed.

The family gathered around him, looking on at first in shock and sadness, and then utter surprise.

Then he opened his eyes. 'Hello you,' he said. 'Why the sad face?'

I sobbed in sheer relief that we'd been given another chance, as he arose from what had seemingly been no more than a deep sleep in his favourite chair.

But I didn't really buy that. I just knew that something quite magical must have happened. All of our guests were either applauding or cheering, while the man in the white floppy hat smiled angelically and gently placed his hand on my shoulder.

'Nobody here will have to leave this world tonight. Not on my watch,' he said. Then he vanished into the night air.